UBOA ACT 3

UBOA ACT 3

Prince Otchere

First Printing,
September 15, 2025

This book is dedicated to my late father Peter, my mother Leticia, my wife Cheri, my children Prince, Malaika, and Cameron. Also, to my family friends and close supporters. Thank you.
"We Give God the Glory."

CONTENTS

The Intervention pt.2

Adam arrived home walking towards the entrance of his cave just in time to hear the faint but agonizing moans his mate. Immersed in feeding their hungry child, the creature took little notice of Adam moving thru the entranceway. He stopped short of his tracks to observe of his mate disregarding the laws which he had set in place. It was then in the dark shadows that Adam decided to allow his fears to play out, he watched on with tempered indifference as the child drank from the bosoms of his malnourished mother.

The famished child fed eagerly from his mother's bosoms offering little concern to the condition and health of his parent. Cain with his small finger clutched to his mother's bosoms devouring and feeding away at the faint and feeble body. Adam looked on with pity and disappointment. He motioned disagreeably, somewhat irritated by his mate's act of disobedience and lack of compliance. He watched remotely from the entranceway as his beloved companion began to grow pasty, and pale almost ghastly in appearance.

Adam was filled with anxiety and concern but held back against the urge to intervene. He was upset by his mate's deliberate disregard of his recommendations. Adam feeling slighted and irritated decided to allow for natural consequences of subornation to run its course. However, at viewing his partner in such a dire and crippling state did not provide Adam the satisfaction he imagined. Seeing the fragile image of his feeble and malnourished mate confined to a helpless state. This was truly a sore sight for Adam to behold. The child's insatiable hunger seemed illogical in comparison to its small frame. Cain displayed a gluttonous appetite and desire appearing indifferent to his father's incredulous assessment paying little mind to the surveying onlooker. Cain continued to clench tightly to the breasts of his mother suckling hard from the defenseless creatures' teats.

The newborns chiseled nails pierced the soft skin of it's his mother's chest. The pain prompted a muffled outcry that caused Adam to feel pity and remorse for his mate. He found the feeding to be painfully unbearable to watch. Adam stepped out from the shadows of the doorway and drawing closer he found his mate's face soaked with tears. The fact of the matter became apparently clear that a life brought into this world carried the potential to rid and extinguish the very essence and life force of its matron. Unconcerned with the moans and groans of his fatigued mother the small creature seemed determined if not eager to remove breath and life from his mother.

Cain continued to drink freely from the tired and exhausted body of his ailing mother. The poor creature lay paralyzed and stoic staring off into the bleak abyss of nothingness. His mate watched on helpless to respond or act as the parasite like child continued to feed with little concern or regard. It became suddenly apparent to Adam realizing that if left unchecked the famished child would consume his maker and bring an end of creature. "Nooo!" Adam shouted running quickly to his mate's side to offer aide and support. Adam moved rather swiftly in his intervention and managed to interject himself between his mate and child. He wrestled to pull Cain away from the grips and clutches of his mother bosoms. The forceful removal amid suction caused a jolting explosion of warm milk to spew out and discharge onto the floor.

It didn't take long before Cain began to express his displeasure giving out a loud and wailing cry. The outcry was deafening and seemed to increase. The action only helped to further Adam's irritation, and growing frustration. "What kind of creature are you!" Adam yelled out reacting short tempered and inpatient. "Do you not see that you are hurting your poor mother!" The frightened, and helpless child answered back instinctively with an amplified screams that blared beyond his usual outcries. Adam struggled to regain his composure recalling on the fact that Cain was an infant and incapable of rational thought, or reasoning. "Had I not been hasty and waited a moment longer," Adam paused dreading the thought. "You would have ended your mother's life and removed from this world the companion and source of joy.

Cain's loud cries, and shrieks were accompanied by a flurry of tears. The cries echoed and filled the small cavern room. The shrieking wails of the child was loud enough to pierce the ears and stir the nerves of his mother. Adam mate was beginning to slowly awaken and regain consciousness. The high pitch sound of helpless wailing proved nearly impossible for any mother to ignore. Adam watched with growing remorse and empathy as his mate struggle to sit up. The pain of labor and childbirth made it difficult for his partner to maneuver or move while in a debilitating state.

Adam's mate mustering what little energy remained managed to raise a brow in search of the crying child. Looking around for the infant child Adam's partner was instantly gripped with fear. The new mother began to panic frantically searching about wildly until finally locating the crying newborn in the possession and care of his father. Looking on at his mate's face, Adam felt unsettled by the tearful glare of his mate. The look of sadness and worry drawn over his partners face helped to extinguish the temper of his fiery ego. Beneath the watchful eye of his partners gaze Adam appeared tamed and remorseful for his crude conduct and behavior.

Adam altered his demeanor and cradled the crying child in between his arms before nestling the infant across his chest. It was as though Adam was affected somewhat unhinged by his mate's resilience and display of affection. Adam witnessed first-hand the supernatural force of motherhood displayed through the unselfish act and need to protect and care for their young. The power and prowess of his mate was enough to simmer Adams hot boiling nerves to a cold frigid temperature. It was not long before the loud wailing of the young child began to simmer and quiet down.

Adam sensing that Cain was approaching sleep began slowly rocking back and forth to ensure that the child was fully settled. It did not take very long for the small child to concede. Cain produced an exhausting yawn that indicated without question that the small infant had fallen asleep. In that moment and instance while holding his son in his arms Adam was overcome by the intimacy of their bond. "I am sorry son." Adam whispered, "It was unfair of me to raise my voice and yell. Especially when you have done nothing wrong in your desire for food and sustenance."

Adam caressed his sons back with the tips of his fingers softly scrolling across the infants spinal bones. He admired all the tiny pieces and tender muscles that held the small frame of the creature intact. "It was simply idiotic of me to believe that you my child could be a creature of malevolence. I beg that you find in your tiny heart a way to forgive me." The humming sound of snoring indicated that Adam's plea had fallen on deaf ears as Cain was now fast asleep.

Adam walked slowly over to his mate and gently placed the child back into the arms of his mother restoring the natural union. Silence fell over the room as the couple gazed softly into each other eyes. The daunting and overly exhausting day was now nearly complete with the triad of souls sharing in a moment of intimacy and sacredness. It was truly a picturesque image to behold. Adam was tired and exhausted from the toils of the day and chose to rest beside his child and partner. Adam found comfort in the warm reception he received being welcomed by the open arms of his mate and child. He coiled his body around the body of his mate caressing the face of his partner with gentle strokes and delicate soft touches.

In overcoming their first obstacle and challenge the family demonstrated fortitude and resilience. The synergy between love and joy unified in the glowing faces of Adam and his mate. The admiration and affection shared between the two lovers was pure and true. The tender somewhat encapsulating moment captured if nothing else the ideals of love tailored with innocence and compassion. The rarest of portraits was the brushed image of first nuclear family shone vibrantly over a gentle canvas stroked with love.

As Adam held his child and mate in his arms his mind began to wander. He began to consider how impactful the terrifying experience had been. The moment exposed Adam to a fearful truth that the success of their livelihood and existence was now intertwined and dependent of each other for survival. The hierarchy of human connectedness which forms like chains linking and binding creatures together not just by blood but by way of love and caring for one another. The birth of Adam's understanding and growth marked a transformative moment for him. The priceless lessons garnered through parenting were invaluable despite the obvious risk outweighing the reward.

The image of Adam lying peacefully with his family was truly a picturesque and serene. Had the image been captured it would fetch a lucky artist a lofty prize and sum. Throughout history these rewards have been pursued and sought after by artisans hoping to capture the rare moment using tools of precision, skill, depth, and detail in their interpretations and replications of this tender and heartwarming moment. However, only a few visionaries have ever come close to encapsulating and depicting in various fashions and art-forms the embodiment of harmony unity and love shared between Adam and his family. The complexities of such an illustration would serve especially difficult for those inexperienced or lacking in empathy and compassion.

The Intervention pt. 3

The intimate moment was truly enthralling as Adam was viewed holding his mate, and child. Adam straddled his arms comfortably around the sleeping pair nestling them into a more suitable and comfortable position. Despite the presence of overwhelming love and compassion that filled the space it would not be enough to facilitate his partners recovery. In his palms Adam could feel the damp moistness of his mate's body increase feverishly. Perspiration and dew began to form over the creature's glossy face. Small beads of sweat began to trickle and run down the contours of his partners back.

A brisk chill of cool air beneath his arm caused Adam to withdraw his grip and hold over his mates heated body. It became undoubtedly clear that his mate was morbidly observing his partners quaking and quivering lips. The plum and youthful face of his mate; once filled with life and vigor was now dreary and dampened with gloom. The flux of changing symptoms ranging from hot to cold provoked tremors and shakes that left the trembling creature grounded. The clattering sound of crashing teeth drew alarm and concern prompting Adam to recall the golden apple. "The apple." he quickly reminded himself drawing a sense of relief at the thought.

Adam had forgotten to present the gift of the golden apple which he obtained from Tree. In the absentminded realization that he had dropped the apple during the encounter. He had lost track of the fruit somewhere between if not near the corridor of the cavern entranceway. Adam's eyes flashed every inch of the caved room, in search of the golden apple. He searched about aimlessly in dire peril before finally locating the apple on the ground near the wall. Adam moved without haste and dashed rather quickly to retrieve the apple.

He managed with little effort to secure the apple and return to his lovers' side. He was nervous and filled with uncertain questions on how he would apply and administer the apple to his enfeebled companion. His partner was now soaked and drenched in sweat while quivering dangerously. Adam placed the head of his lover over his lap, and with his palms he began to wipe away the pool of moist sweat. He drew in breath and began to blow cool air over his partners face. Adam sucked in the air around him, inhaling deeply and storing it beneath the depths of his lungs. He held the air briefly before exhaling and releasing the cool breath of air over the face and body of his mate. Adam repeated the act numerous times before reaching exhaustion. His efforts did not go in vain as the exasperating actions helped to cool down his mate and avoid the severe symptoms of crippling heat.

Adam held his ailing companion in his arms, speaking soft and gentle words into his partner ears. He struggled desperately to hold back his own tears as he comforted his mate. The onset of emotions that flushed over Adams face eventually spewed from his eyes dampening his mouth and face. Adam sniffled ceaselessly wiping away the thick wad of mucus running down and over his lips. The grotesque and unsavory image of Adam was unusual in stature and difficult to recognize. Defaced by fear and uncertainty Adam desperately clung to his partner with partner. He placed his lovers face gently near his own and began a most passionate and heartfelt plea for his partner to awaken. "Please my love, do not die." Adam cried out, "Do not desert me." He displayed the golden apple firmly clasped in his hand. "You must eat this apple," he urged placing the fruit over the lips and mouth of his mate. However, the enfeebled creature would not bite or eat from the apple. The frail condition of his mate had left the creature feeling much too weak to bite or take in a morsel of the golden apple.

"Please my love." Adam pleaded mercilessly conscious and aware of the time drawing near. Every minute deemed precious; every second seem more vital than the last. Adam tried desperately to hold back the growing sense of hopelessness that was beginning to surface in his thoughts. "You must attempt at the very least to eat from the apple, and in doing so you will reclaim your health." His partner could hear Adam as he spoke and trying desperately to fulfill his request invited the apple closer for another attempt. Adam brought the apple closer once again to the brim of his partner's mouth. Holding the fruit over his mate's face despite the effort his partner was still unable to bite or chew from the apple. Adam felt sympathetic towards his mate observing his partners wavering attempt to gnaw and nibble at the fruit. Despite the effort his mate was unable to puncture or penetrate the hardened exterior of the golden apple.

Adam was overly distraught by the challenge faced before him. He caressed his brows in deep thought and heavy consideration as to how he could aide his sick and dying partner. It wasn't long before a somewhat uncomfortable and nauseating idea appeared at the forefront of his mind. Adam was pensive and contemplated for some time on the proper course of action. He struggled somewhat with the revolting thought, and idea that filled his mind. Adam drew disgust and uneasiness from the very notion however, he was desperate and scarcely running out of time. Left with no alternative means or resolutions Adam bit forcefully into golden apple and began chewing. Adam crushed the soft fruit between his teeth until it was fully pasteurized into mush. Adam gathered the food between his lips and softly pressed his mouth against his partner's mouth. He used his tongue to deliver and feed the apple directly into his partner's mouth.

The strange idea was conceived out of fear and sheer desperation. Adam adopted the strange practice after witnessing many of the feathery birds feeding their young in the same manner. Adam blushed with embarrassment remembering how he once held a personal prejudice against the repulsing act. He described the foul act as "repulsing, and utterly distasteful." However, in the moment Adam would abandon his childhood prejudices. He could only see the face of his beloved partner rapidly approaching death. With little time to spare Adam bit once again from the apple and chewed it quickly in his mouth. He pureed the apple between his teeth, mushing and mashing the tasty fruit while trying not to swallow the sweet, and tasty fruit. When ready Adam applied the soft food in between the jaws of his mate's lips.

To the untrained eye the exchange between Adam and his mate would resemble that of an intimate if not passionate kiss. It was difficult to determine whether the exchange of affection between lovers emerged from desperation or necessity, or possibly both. Crouched in close facing the delicate face of his partner, Adam kissed his mate passionately using his tongue once again to pass the chewed apple into his mate's mouth. Afterwards he massaged his lovers' throat to help the creature take down and swallow the pasteurized food. Adam too began to feel the restorative effects of the golden apple taking subtle notice to the sudden increase in his health.

A full rejuvenation of his body would have taken place had Adam chosen to bite from the apple and devour the tasty apple himself. His only hope was that he was not too late to save his mate from a fatal end. The chilling thought alone caused his nerves to tremble and shake frantically. An overwhelming feeling of helplessness began to spawn within the shadowy corners of his mind. Adam being strong minded and resilient refused to allow his indignation and fears to overcome him, "I will not cower while my mate suffers," Adam asserted himself aggressively, "I shall not allow the eternal footman to hold captive my mate not without first waging war." Adam declared his proclamation with conviction and self-determination.

Adam's honorable words courageous and uplifting seem to manifest and take hold of his body as he quickly took another bite from the chunky apple and was back again at his lover's lips. Adam moved autonomously imploring a swift rhythmic approach in his actions and movements. He bit, chewed, kissed, and then proceeded to repeat the act. It was not long before Adam discovered that he had nearly devoured a large portion of the golden apple. Adam paused his efforts briefly to observe whether the treatment being provided was making a positive impact and improvement on his patient.

Adam searched desperately over his mate's face for an indication of life. He examined the creature condition for any signs of improved vitality in his partner. However, in spite all of Adam valiant efforts the circumstances seem bleak and disappointing for his partner. The daunting effort and fight for his mate's life now seem futile and lost. It sickened Adam to look down at his companion in such a grimly state. He felt emotionally stiffened and empty with no resolution or resolve in the unfortunate matter. Adam sat stoically silent appearing desensitized and detached beneath the weight of misery and trouble. Lost within the vast void of his own thoughts Adam attempted to repair his nerves and collect his composure.

The agonizing emotions seemed to sit against cavity and frame of Adam's chest. The humbling experience forced Adam to accept defeat after coming face to face with his fears. Adam begged and pleaded with showering tears for his love to awaken and rise from the deep slumber. however, his partner did not move or budge from the ground laying stiff, and lifeless. Adam's was fraught with misery and anguish over the severed heartbreak. The fountains of his eyes began to moisten and fill up with dew. Adam attempted to hold back the wave of swelling tears forming over his eyes. However, a single teardrop that managed to break free and spool down the creased path of Adams face.

The defiant teardrop had escaped and now treading down the base of Adams face and chin. The lonely teardrop rolled down the side of Adam's lean face navigating an uncharted course and patchy trail. The single tear stopped short after reaching the edge and brim of Adams chin. The nervous tear behaved as though frightened of dip and fall ahead and clung desperately to avoid plummeting. Perched beneath the chiseled structure of his jawline the brave teardrop settled beneath the edge of Adams chin. The clever teardrop would have gladly hung for eternity had it not been for the flurry of tears that followed behind like rainfall.

Melancholy air began to fill the room with gloom and despair. The nauseating stench of misery and turmoil began to fill the room. The combination of negative emotions cast a dark shadow into their home. The air surrounding Adam appeared rather dismal and void of light. It seemed that the death had swung his scepter and allowed for gusty winds of bereavement to breach the fortress of their home. Drawn in by the flickering flame of dwindling light. Death stood silently over Adam waiting patiently to collect on the bounty and warrant of his partner. Strangely the very room that housed Adam's faith would become the tomb and shrine in which he would lay his hopes and dreams to rest. Adam felt very much isolated and alone more than ever before, even the walls themselves seem to betray him expanding in distance. He sat front and center beneath the dimming spotlight of sorrowful tears.

Looking around Adam caught sight of his son and quickly darted to the boy's side. Cain was still asleep unaware of the great misfortune that had just taken place. "Our small child will eventually awaken to discover the unfortunate demise of his mother." Adam thought, "When he is no longer able to suckle and drink from the nourishing bosoms of his mother." Adam was plagued by a host of intrusive thoughts and images that flashed into his mind. He was burdened with the daunting yet dutiful task of burying the lifeless bodies of his beloved family.

"How will I manage to keep our son alive." Adam wept woefully. "When I have nothing to offer to sustain him." Adam struggled with the heart wrenching thought of his partners demise and very soon found his face drenched with moist tears. Salty tears began to roll slowly down the side of Adam face moving down his narrow chin. The trail of tears dripped down over the dry dead body of his unresponsive mate. Adams tears fell like a brisk shower of rain over the body of his befallen mate.

What happened next inside the cavern den was unexplainable to say the least, and nothing short of a miracle. Suddenly without warning the lamed body of his mate began to jerk and stir. Adam rejoiced with excitement believing that the power of his unyielding love had triumphed in the matter. He attributed his partners recovery to the lethargic onset of the potent apple. The slow acting formula had a delayed effect however it was useful in alluding his mate from the fatal hands of death. The watery tears that dripped from Adams eyes fell gently onto his mate's face like warm rain on a hot sultry day. Each watery drop felt more replenishing and inviting than the last. The once befallen creature was now revived posturing beneath the strange climate of Adam's weathering tears. The storm of tears bathed over his mate like a drenching rainstorm. The drops of tears that fell provoked his partners eyes to blink and twitch repeatedly. Adam rejoiced happily in observing animation and movement from his mate. He accepted the twinges, and twitches as promising signs indicating that his mate still reserved a yearning desire to thrive.

"Thank God," Adam praised instinctively, he stopped himself suddenly after catching the truth of his own words. He struggled with the idea being somewhat of an uncomfortable thought. Adam deflected the questionable contempt he harbored towards his father choosing to focus his attention back to his mate. "You are alive!" Adam rejoiced peering into the eyes of his beloved mate. The image of the frightened couple bound together in each other's arms help to illustrate the tender moment. Adam embraced his partner tenderly their faces meshed in closeness. "I would never have forgiven myself," Adam began to sob, "had you..." He found himself unable to speak out or declare the fatal words. The dreadful thought caused heartache and brought sickness to his stomach. Adam attempted to help his mate sit up however the partner was still much too weak to move or stand. The recovery process for such a feeble and paralyzing condition would undoubtedly require much time and patience.

Adam discouraged against any sudden movements or attempts to get up. "Be still," Adam reassured his partner, "Do not try to sit up for your body is much too frail." Adam comfortably propped his partners head over his legs. "Do not worry," Adam assured his partner clutching the remaining portion of the golden apple. He quickly wiped away any dirt and debris from the fruit before gently placing the apple against the lips of his mate.

"Bite down." Adam encouraged. "Eat the remainder of apple and be well again." Adam pled whole heartedly. His partner still enfeebled and depleted of energy struggled to open and unhinge its jaw. There was motion in his partners movements however sluggish and slow. Adam watched in growing suspense at the gradual progression while simultaneously providing affirmation and encouragement to his mate. He rooted on until finally his partner bit into the apple. "Yes!" Adam rejoiced and cheered outwardly. "You will be well soon." Adam declared as he held out the apple to his partners mouth for another bite. The creature bit once again into the fruit, this time in a much livelier manner. The progressive healing powers of the golden apple was beginning to have a noticeable effect over the exhausted and tiresome couple.

Adam observed his partner appearing livelier by the minute. He watched on in amazement at the transformation unfolding before him. The dim light of fatigue and exhaustion that was masked his partner face began to slowly disappear. The transformation seemed almost magical to Adam in witnessing the regenerative process. Adam rejoiced watching his mate returning to good health and homeostasis. He was happy and rather ecstatic to see his partners eyes fresh and clear as pearls. His partners face began to flush with color indicating a slow and subtle return to vigor and life. Staring down into the face his mate Adam was overcome with a scaling range of emotions.

Adam rejoiced at the sight of his companion and dearest friend being able to draw breath again. He was enthusiastically relieved to have his mate and partner back at his side. Adam was overcome with excitement and joy to say the least and sat in silent anticipation watching his mate slowly recover. Adam looked at his mate with growing optimism as the creature's appearance began to improve before his eyes. Astonishingly the enfeebled corpse like figure of his mate no longer seemed ghastly in appearance, but instead began to bloom with vitality and life. Adam offered his mate another bite from the apple, but the gentle creature refused his offer deeming it unnecessary. His mate declined the apple and moved the remainder of the fruit towards Adam's face. Adam mate rested the sweet morsel over the brim of his lips, and with a nod encouraged him to bite. Adam did as implied and bit effortlessly from the ripened fruit devouring the remains of the golden apple that would ensure his strength and good health.

In the silent den among a reflection of smiles the three creatures held firmly to one-another in a deep embracing gesture. The warmth of touching bodies ensued a reassuring calm over Adam. He had never been happier than at this moment. The reception of soaked, and dampened faces brought comfort over their reunification. Adam developed a higher value and understanding for love viewing the intense emotion as being extremely powerful and potent. Adam believed that with enough love, one could wield the ability to move mountains, or part oceans. And in this case love could revive the dead and return them to the world of the living.

The tender moment was a would be forever engrained in his heart, and mind. In a few days time the two lovers would be fully recover and overcome their ailments. The nearly fatal experience was traumatic and would forever remain a blemish stain in Adams memory. Adam and his mate radiated a pure and unselfish love which at the time was rare and highly desired. Those who have been fortunate to discover and experience the rarest of antiquities are highly favored and truly blessed. Adam would need to safeguard the gift of abundance and favor he received. The act of protecting his newly found fortune and treasure would not be an easy feat as Adam will eventually come to discover.

The Scavenger

As time went on Adam grew more adapt in assuming the role and position of patriarch of his family. He became the adhesive glue that fastened and held the family bond. Adam was the backbone and spine of his family exuding strength in his ideals and provisioning. Adam taught his family the sacred geometry of the world, imparting basic knowledge and wisdom pertaining to the chemistry and fundamentals of life.

"Man will love his mate and child," Adam shared with his family, "but he can never love them equally. It is the triangulation of interconnectedness." Adam attempted to explained, "When love is observed and requited between lovers, then love will overflow and spill over to the child." Adam turned his head gently to meet the face his son, Adam began to address his son speaking rather candidly to the small child. "At present it appears that affection and nourishment are your only regard and concern. It is why you favor, and cling happily at your mother's side. However, you will eventually outgrow the desire of affection and will yearn for something much greater than your nurturing mother can provide."

Cain was still young and understood basic commands. He was unable to decipher the blatant context of his father's lengthy ramblings and teachings. The provisional nourishment received by the small child went unaccounted and absent of gratuity or gratitude of any kind. Adam learned to accept that the need for sustenance can make a child develop and grow bias and impartial to the strange conditioning. He observed the judgment natural development of his son demonstrating preferential treatment and favoritism towards his matron. Adam witnessed firsthand the very dynamic and development between mother and child take place. He observed with civil patience as his son entered and overcome the early stages of childhood development. Adam watched with cautionary lenses as the young child's infatuation with his mother began to slowly dwindle. Despite Adams singular perception of his son, Cain was naturally divergent and equipped to shift his love bilaterally. He occasionally flashed the beacon of light and love over his father which often improved his mood.

An entire season passed since Adam's last visit to see Tree. Although he returned once to thank Tree for her kindness his visit was short and abrupt. Adam prolonged the visit by keeping himself very much busy. He allocated much of his time and energy to upholding provisional obligation to his family. The responsibility was a task that Adam took much pleasure in fulfilling. Every morning Adam would set out to scavenge the rural area in search of nourishment and provision. The scavenger lifestyle would introduce the family to a different lifestyle and way of living. Adam and his companion as well as child had become delightfully accustomed to the taste of flamed and broiled foods. The introduction of meat into their diets occurred in response to hunger and necessity. The nutritional change demonstrated the family's ability to survive and thrive in foreign and unfamiliar environments.

Adam was beginning to settle into his role and position as provider and protector to his family. Life on the outside was becoming more manageable for Adam however it did not compare to life in the garden. Adam recalled the bountiful land of Eden housing endless pastures and fruits of various options. He ruminated over the fertile estate which produced and harvested fruits and vegetables to support and sustain nourishment. Eden was unlike like the dry and desolate wasteland which sheltered the most grotesque and detestable of God's creations. These outcasts being mostly carnivorous creatures largely scavenger type roamed freely. Unbeknown to Adam at the time was that these very creatures would later come to serve as a source of protein and nourishment for his family. The sudden change in diet caused issues unforeseen issues with digestion. Initially what started off as somewhat of an uncomfortable introduction and change in diet soon became tolerated and accepted as norm. Adam and his family were going from a natural diet consisting mostly of fruits and berries to consuming heavy protein of meat and fat.

Outside the great walls amongst the barren wasteland there was no fertile land or soil to produce or plants vegetation. Meat was the only source of nourishment within the two-hundred-yard circumference of their home. Adam relished for a moment over his childhood and laughed at the thought somewhat rather amused. He recalled his prepubescent discretions against eating vegetables, he remembered the daunting look on Tree's face as she would attempt to feed him vegetation of any kind. Tree would often grow frustrated and overwhelmingly perplexed and annoyed by young Adam's mischievous defiance in refusing to eat or finish his meals. Adam chuckled to himself reflecting on how his childish behavior and opposition was the primary source of Tree's anxiety and stress. These warm reflections of his upbringing brought a smile, and calm over Adam that help to rejuvenate his sense of growth and purpose.

It was Adams purpose to provide for his family, and so every day he would set out in search of game to bring home to his family. Adam was no expert hunter his instincts of survival were primitive at best. However, he learned quickly mastering skills and techniques that at first seemed somewhat unnatural and unorthodox. The pampered comforts of his youthful upbringing and the life that he once enjoyed could not be found out here in the forgotten and forsaken wastelands. The narrowing river hole was not blue or clear like the rivers that ran through Eden. The unfiltered water outside of paradise was murky and rather putrid in taste. Still the family drank from the river and ate graciously the foods and spoils that Adam scavenged and managed to bring home to ensure their survival.

Their new lives seemingly low in station was no paradise or haven for them. Eden seemed like an oasis when compared to the desolate wastelands they now chartered and called their home. "This new world," Adam referenced regularly during his teachings, "will not be easy for us, but together we will sustain." His bold words offered a sense of reassurance and comfort to his family reaffirming his established role as the executive director and proprietor of his home.

Adam grew up accustomed to being a dependent often relying on the assistance support and of Tree as his caregiver and matriarch. This time however, it was Adam who would assume the role and position of provider and protector which filled him with drive and determination to master the challenges set before him.

Adam's first challenge and priority was to learn how to become a provider for his family. He often scoured and scavenged over the foreign lands searching for provisions and useful tools to source at his disposal. The area which surrounded their home was vast and mostly uncharted territory. This mysterious new world was full of wild new creatures, brute beasts with raging tempers. "Beasts and savages." Adam often referred to the creatures living outside of Eden. He could not imagine Eden housing such enormous, and gargantuan creatures. They were untamed and mischievous creatures that carried on without law or any form of governing. It came as no surprise to Adam why these creatures like himself had been removed and excommunicated from Eden.

Adam witnessed on several occasions as the larger creatures prayed on the smaller weaker creatures. The strange and bizarre pecking order seemed to be the way of life out in the common lowlands. In observing the ways of the savage culture Adam began to study the strange customs of the brute beasts. He studied their behavior in search of redeeming qualities that would exonerate them from their present circumstances however, he could find none. At the end of Adam's extensive study, he concluded with a mental log accounting for the various inhabitants. He began by organizing and grouping the savage creatures arranging them from least threatening to the most dangerous. Having already accepted the natural order of this new land Adam was prepared if not determined to secure his rightful place at the pinnacle of the competitive food chain.

There dwelled many savage creatures of formidable sizes, large monstrous beasts with shearing teeth as long as daggers. Their sharp claws keenly edged could easily shred the flesh and hide of any creature that dare to challenge or oppose them. Watching over the creatures studying them close Adam noticed how grotesque and boorish these creatures appeared. The savage creatures were aesthetically primitive and unappealing unlike the animals and mammals that inhabited Eden. "These creatures of the wild," Adam thought himself, "could easily butcher and make prey of the residents of Eden with little effort or difficulty."

Adam never dared to challenge the behemoth sized creatures that prowled about the yards of the wastelands. He instead searched for his rightful place within the massive pecking order near the base and bottom. Adam thought it best to engage with only the smaller, and less aggressive of the savages. The logical decision and inclination would serve him in is goals of self-preservation which was Adams highest priority. His rationale and hope at the time was to minimize any unforeseen dangers and lessen likelihood of sustaining a fatal injury. Adam assumed the smaller savage creatures would be easier target and marks for prey, when compared to their larger more aggressive predecessors. Adam's logic reflected the fact that he was still unskilled posing as a novice amateur in the sport of hunting. The sport of capturing game was a new arena for Adam who decided it best to begin at a modest pace in accordance with his skill level and experience.

Adam's first set of tools for hunting was an arsenal of rocks and stones for which he used to fling ferociously at smaller creatures. The sheer force and impact of the fling would ultimately determine the fate of its victim. If flung with enough force, and velocity the rock could kill if not stun its victim depending on the creature's size. It took some time before Adam fully skilled in the art of stoning. However, his initial attempts at hunting concluded without success. Adam was unlucky in finding a lamed creature willing to pose long enough for him to strike down.

The first few days while still adjusting to the new setting and environment. Adam learned to scavenge and often brought home food containing mostly scraps and unfinished remains left behind by one of the savage beasts. Adam would often retrieve the left over remains and bring the morsel back to his family. The uncovering of half-eaten corpses served as a joyous occasion for Adam. It signified the promise of a meal for his family and more importantly a day void of danger and unnecessary risks. Adam's only complaint was that he did not find fresh corpses more often. That night his family enjoyed the spoils of a fierce and intense battle. The likes of which Adam and his family gladly offered their gratitude and thanks.

The practice of scavenging was quickly becoming an art in which Adam dedicated much of his time. He came to own several rocks of which he attributed a sense of showmanship. Adam piled the stones in his home like trophies each rock significant and purposeful in affirming his fatal conquests. The evening hours was when the family gathered to commune often coming together to feast and share in the bounty of Adam's capture and prey. It was during these intimate meals when Adam would openly share tales, and stories of his exploits all of which his family drew fascination and admiration from his heralding tales.

Adam shared with his family the different strategies and various tactics and skills he employed being out in the wilderness. He boasted with unwavering confidence about his growing abilities and skills as a scavenger nomad. Adam shared that his aim and precision enabled him to hit targets within range and distance. He saw himself was slowly elevating from the ranks of a scavenger to likes of a hunter and was becoming less reliant on scraps and left over foods to feed his family. Adam was beginning to bring home moderately sized meals home to his family.

Adam was slowly developing into the hunter and full-fledged warrior that he envisioned himself to be. His impressive skill of rock slinging brought nourishment to his family on a nightly basis. And though in the beginning his prey appeared small it was enough to sustain and quell the appetite and hunger of his mate and growing child. The ability to provide for his family filled Adam with a glowing sense of pride, and purpose. Adam felt good knowing that he was very much capable of sustaining the health and life of his family.

One morning while out hunting Adam encountered a savage boar along his path. The creature lay dying alongside the dirty paved pathway. The boorish beast was near its death with its body severely battered and badly bruised. It looked as though the creature had been trampled by a massive stampede of parading beasts. The injury appeared rather fatal seeing as the creature's bones were snapped and broken from the impact. There was a large gash and wound stretching across the creature's side. It's rib cage and plate bones were exposed and made sightly visible. The graphic and somewhat gruesome image was a rather eerie and uncomfortable sight for Adam to stomach.

A swarm of flies hovered over the dying creature while a swarm of insects began to surround the corpse ready to make an easy lunch of the fallen creature. Adam took notice to a long-jagged bone protruding through the creature hide and flesh. The sharped edged bone would become the inspiration for which Adam would use to create a new tool. Adam planned to drag the corpse home and strip the creature of its bones. The creature's death though untimely would set precedence to a new stage and frontier for innovation. Upcycled and repurposed the creatures' bones would provide Adam with a new set of sharp tools to support in his goal and purpose of ensuring his family's survival.

Adam proposed the idea to his mate suggesting that such tools could serve beneficial and useful in their daily lives. Adam's partner found the sharp bones useful in scaling and shearing foods making the work less daunting. The sharp jagged bones would soon become Adam's the preferred weapon and hunting tool. He began to use and rely more frequently on the sharp bones to increase his kills. The sharped edged tools were useful in penetrating the thick skin and hide of his prey. Adam maintained the jagged bones often chiseling and sharpening his tools well enough to puncture and pierce the hide and skin of any creature that dare to defy or challenge him. Adam was becoming more skilled as a hunter and was adept to gathering food for his family. His mate who was always supportive and appreciative of Adams endeavors took part in the process by offering to treat and cure the meat before preparing it over a fiery flame. The act of transforming slabbed meat into a delicious family meal was remarkable work. Adam shared with family his ambitious dreams of owning a set of sharpened tools designed especially for gaming. He was surprised if not very much pleased by his partners ingenuity and ability to forge the very tools in which Adam had described. His mate with the assistance of their child worked together to forge sharp daggers and create pointy objects from the bones and remains of the savage creatures.

Cain watched his parents together interaction, observing his father's glowing appreciation for his mother upon receiving the first primitive knife. The daggering tool proved especially inspiring to Adam who began to consider a host of sizable challengers and contenders coming to mind. In practice the tool served exceptionally well in helping Adam to slay and takedown his victims with ease and little effort. It would seem the method of using one creature's bone to slay and disarm another larger much superior creature was working tactfully.

What started as a one boar's knife quickly grew to include a catalogue of sharp staffs, and multiple spears. It was no doubt that Adam, was truly developing in the art and skill of hunting and scavenging prey. It wouldn't take very long before Adam began challenging creatures whose stature and girth resembled his very own and often twice folds. A sense of excitement filled Adam's nerves whenever he conquered or overpowered his opponent in a fierce battle. Adam shared tales of his exhibitions and exploits while declaring the sharp instruments as redeeming and empowering tool. "I now enjoy the challenge," Adam confessed openly before his family "and no longer view these large savages as adversaries but rather formidable opponents gifted with unmatched strength and agility. However powerful as the savages may appear the savages lack intellect and reasoning, and that is our leverage." Adam explained reserving a sense of superiority in his tone. "The bigger the savage beast, the greater the challenge and resistance. Mostly impenetrable and well-guarded bearing coats and layers of thicket skins." Adam enjoyed talking to his family about the exploits of his encounters out in the field. If left unchecked he could go on all day speaking of his many experiences hunting wild game. "The smaller ones," looking directly into the face of his small son, and drawing near, "are far too easy." He teased jabbing playfully. "Stab!" Cain Jumped up falling out of his startled by his father banter. Smiling down at his son, Adam helped Cain back up. "My apologies son, I was simply demonstrating the impact of the powerful tool when applied in combat, however I allowed my imagination to get run away with me."

Young Cain listened to his father stories with admiration, and respect. The dramatic details of his father's heroism were often exaggerated and embellished by the unreliable narrator. Stories of Adam's conquests had become a prized source of joy and entertainment for the young boy. Cain often listened to these tales with enchantment and wonderment in his eyes. The young lad would eagerly jump onto his father lap glowing with anticipation at the chance to hear his father tell his heralding tales of adventure. In Cain eyes his father was no mortal man but rather supernatural being resembling the likeness of a God or demigod whichever deemed appropriate.

Adam attempted to instill pride into his son often reminding Cain of his family's lineage and origin. He shared tales of a life and a world unfamiliar to the small boy. Adam ruminated on better times before settling as outcasts amongst the unmerciful lands. Adam placed the seeds of family and heritage into the soft fertile mind of his son with the hopes that those very seeds would someday bloom and grow. There were many bedtime stories told by Cain with references to Eden and its bountiful beauty. Adam would confess inwardly his biggest regret was that his son would never see or lay eyes on the leafy green pastures within Eden's wall.

Young Cain saw his father like many children at his age as possessing unquestionable strength and powers of invincibility. He did not dispute or challenge his father's bravery, and heroic exploits. He believed whole heartedly the daily regimen of tales and epic battles endorsed by Adam waged against some unfortunate creature. Adam was unaware at the time the lasting impact and the sort of impression that his stories were beginning to have on young Cain's developing mind. These stories and more help to reinforce an image of truth about his father. One that would ultimately shape his overall understanding and definition and of manhood.

The conquests in Adam's stories yielded some truth as he often returned home the victor of the grueling sport he now regarded as hunting. Adam thought very little of the consequences that his embellished tales could possibly cause other than bringing the look of joy and excitement into the eyes and face of his son. Adam did not foster any shame or guilt in romanticizing the parts of his life he considered menial or trifle. He managed somehow to elongate the facts of his day by weaving together the misadventures of his day into embellished stories. Adam's short-sighted views found little fault in fantasizing his experiences as a form of entertainment for his family's consumption. Perhaps it was the dulled conditions of the dry desert life, or the ample time Adam spent beneath the hot-tempered sun that caused him to hallucinate and conjure up such fanciful tales. However, Adam was bias and somewhat prejudice in his orations as he did not share or disclose any tales or stories that demonstrated his shortcoming and failures. He was intentional in his absentmindedness seemingly quick to omit or make mention of the many notable blunders and mishaps that occurred while scavenging to his partner and son.

Adam shamefully encased the stories of his shortcomings with ease and convenience. His epic fails and falls were buried deep and secured tightly within the vault of his mind. Convenient amnesia and memory loss prevented Adam from recounting the many failed and embarrassing instances in which misfortune incurred while out hunting. Unheard were the stories of times when Adam would be outwitted by some clever savage or outmatched by some brave and cunning beast. There were many instances of untold moments and challenges encountered by Adam while out hunting. The potent scent of Adam body had become a pungent and familiar aroma among the savaging creatures. His perspiration and sweat would often attract hungry predators determined to turn the tables and make a meal of Adam. The hungry beasts would set chase after Adam sending him scurrying off narrowly escaping danger. Adam would often retreat home in fear for his life, and when questioned or asked to the reason for his hasty arrival home, Adam provided a list of plausible excuses which concealed his fearful retreat. These experiences were vaguely repressed and forgotten memories that Adam conveniently decided not to recall.

Adam believed that disclosing his failures, and shortcoming would only help to portray him as vulnerable in the eyes of his son. He saw no fault in omitting and redacting the unusual and embarrassing tales he believed served no use or favor. Through Adams lenses and frame of thought, he had done no harm. There was no sign of foul play or crime being committed out in the open. Unfortunately, he was unable to see beneath the surface to view the internal mold and impression that his exaggerated stories were having on his son. And as time went on so would Adam's tales of his falsified encounters and conquests. His stories began to grow more gruesome with every retelling.

Adam's orations often went unchecked. This allowed him to conjure up fanciful tales that filled him with as much joy and excitement as it did his family hearing the stories. Adam's uncivil encounters with the beastly creatures of the wild was becoming the family's primary source of amusement and escape from their mundane lives. Adam's detailed countless battles and stories draped in gruesome gore and bloodshed which seem to amuse and entertain Cain the most. He listened attentively to father, his small face and widened eyes stoically tethered to his father's every word. It came as no surprise that whenever Adam attempted to conclude his story time the young prince would plead and throw childish tantrums and fits. Cain reacted explosively by crying out and demanding an encore. He wallowed and pleaded for his father to share another story and tale.

Adam saw no fault in being somewhat imaginative when indulging his son. He embellished his stories like any father called to recount the memorable instances in his life. He defended his behavior by placing the bulk of the blame on his uncontainable affection and fondness for his family. Adam justified the manipulation of his adventures as bending the truth in what he called, "the appropriate direction." Adam's colorful stories helped to nourish and feed his sons appetite and growing curiosity. Cain gathered as much information from the epic tales while taking in as much intel about the world outside of their home.

Adams tales had become to Cain more like the daily briefings filled with current events and updated news of the outside world. The life and world outside of the cavern was beginning to peek Cain's interest. Adam had little insight into the corruption and influence of his stories posed on his son. The incorrigible tales were being accepted and taken somewhat literally by the impressionable child. The projection of Adam stories and tales offered no disclaimer indicating falsehood and exaggerated truths. It would have been best practice if Adam had ended the telling of his gruesome stories as fictional and untrue. Some believed that a warranted disclosure may have possibly helped to derail his son from his inevitable fate.

Please dear reader be gentle and not cruel as it would be infantile for anyone to condemn Adam's parenting, and regard it as poor. It is easy for one to speculate and assume that the gruesome stories that Adam shared with Cain would someway foreshadow the young boy's fate. It would be senseless to chastise the first-time parent with issuances and reprieves unbecoming. I plea that the reader refrain and reserve all judgments until the conclusion and closing of this unauthorized biography

It is important that the reader avoids condemning Adam and remain objective in their personal view of this candid retelling of Adam's life. It is recommended that readers exercise empathy as their guiding principle when reading this work. Allow one's mind and body to transcend time and assume space within the foundational realms of antiquity. Let us pay homage and respect to our dearest patriarch the father of civilization and humanity. Adam was not simply the first man, he was also the first father, parent, and caretaker. He received no instructions or foundational support but managed the best he could with the resources afforded to him. And yet somehow, he managed the extraordinary feat of founding an entire race of species into existence.

The Domestic

Over time Adam would learn to holm his craft as a hunter steadily improving his skills and technique. He no longer viewed himself as being a novice in the primal sport of hunting, but rather a fierce competitor. What began as a means of survival for his family initially forged out of fear and desperation was now an active lifestyle that fueled Adam's competitive spirit and obsessive nature. Adam and his family were not wasteful and learned to reuse and repurpose the mane and hides of the fallen victims. Adams partner took to fashion small pieces of garments and apparel for the family. The primitive garments of clothes were designed to serve as a barrier of protection against the weathering elements. The idea and concept of layering and padding emerged as a safety concern brought forth by their son. Cain drew consideration to the occupational hazards and dangers associated with his father's profession. His love for his father led him to further his mother's design by adding extra layers of padding to Adam's garment to shield and cover his vital parts. The production of these essential garments could not be made possible with the collaboration and support of Adams son and partner.

It became routine that whenever Adam brought home his kill his partner would skin and strip the beast of its hide and mane before preparing their meal. In one corner of the cave their laid piles of furs stretched out like sheets. Amongst the spread were also an assortment of exotic leathers which the family had accumulated and treated to cure over time. The skins of numerous creatures ranging in sizes stacked on top of one another enough as to create a lofty and cozy lounge area in their home. The particularly cushiony space attracted Cain who as a child was naturally drawn to the soft tapestry resting over the variation of different textures. The patterns and shades seem to sooth the young child, peeking his natural inclination and curiosity. He climbed comfortably onto the pallet of soft furs to rest his head. His wandering hands grazed delicately against the matted floor stoking his young and active imagination. Cain saw each different pattern and texture as being purposeful and significant. The collection of manes served as verifiable truth to the stories and tales shared by his father. Cain admired his father fierceness and bravery in overcoming many of his battles and conquests. Adam's toil and sacrifice provided his family a comfortable and modest lifestyle which they had grown accustomed.

Cain could often be found napping on the softest areas of the enmeshed rug. He favored the cozy lounge area because it provided the ideal combination comfort for relaxation. It very soon became his favorite spot and the perfect place for him to take his midday naps. Unbeknown to Cain it would not be long before his private lounge area would become the family's public domain and living room. The soft comfy area would often attract the attention and interest of his mother who often joined alongside him in his naps. Cain very much enjoyed these long intimate and special moment he shared resting alongside his mother. The pile of fur and mane covered the floor padding the ground with softness. The allure of comfort drew the clever duo to commit to draping the boulders and large stones with soft mane and fur to create furnishings. The clever idea of layering mane and hide over rough and jagged rocks helped to transform the large stones into cushiony seating areas. The change appeared to make a significant impact on the overall outlook and aesthetic of their home. The pampered surrounding of the caved dwelling offered the family a comfortable space to relax and enjoy their midday naps.

The decorative improvement of remodeling their home was observed as a direct response to the growing need to pander to their child's development. The provisional benefits of leisure and comfort were extended to Cain by his parents out of desperation and a sense of guilt. Adam and his mate attempted to provide a fraction of the Eden paradise experience onto their child. As an infant Cain was subject to a gentle and easy life afforded to him mostly by his endearing mother. Cains mother demonstrated extra attention to ensure that Cain was comfortable and seldom in need. Highly favored and blessed the young infant, Cain rested comfortably in between the shoulder and bosoms of his endearing parents. However, as he continued to grow develop and grow it became apparent to the parents, Adam especially that Cain was in need his own bed and space. Adam and his mate work together to craft a crib of some using the remains of elongated bones. In the end the finished product of the efforts resembled that of a patchy cage. Despite its rugged composition the pen like structure worked to contain the young child. It would not take long before Adam and his mate would decide to remove the boney bars. The sorrowful sight of Cain crying and wailing in distress was much too unsettling for the new parents. The worn-down area no longer served as a space of peace and tranquility but rather it seemed to cause the young boy distress. Cains mother being overcome with the natural inclinations of a loving parent only desired to provide care and comfort. The unappareled impulse to offer ease and comfort would prompt radicle change and creativity into the creatures in mind.

The rejuvenating idea evoked a sense of excitement within the matriarch. These dormant feelings which were thought to be absent and long forgotten were now being summoned and called forth. Adam's mate thought it best to decorate and adorn the massive cave using the large collection of hides, and furs scattered throughout their home. The decorative remodeling and upkeep of their home would become a domestic obsession and lifelong project for Adams mate. The creative idea began to stoke the fiery embers of his growing ambition. It revealed a deep longing passion within the silent and somewhat melancholy creature. Adam's mate sprang up suddenly as if scorched by the flames of inspiration and motivation. Filled with inspiration and enthusiasm the highly motivated creature was willing to forgo exhaustion and rest until the task was complete Adam's mate worked tirelessly moving about frantically darting back and forth through the cave. The strange and somewhat erratic behavior demonstrated the creatures' frantic efforts to collect and gather the proper and necessary equipment.

The shouldering of such a monumental task would be no easy feat as Adam's mate would soon come to learn. The work and labor that was required caused the creature to enlist the hands and services of the young child. Cain would provide whatever support and assistance that a small boy could offer at the time. Cain was sound asleep before his mother sprang down on him and began stir and shake the sleeping boy to awaken him. Cain awoke to the intrusion of his mother's excitement pleading desperately though a storm of muffled murmurs and hand gestures. Cain's mother attempted desperately to explain and communicate the brilliant idea. Eventually with some time the practice of patience Cain was able to understand most of his mother request and was happy to offer his assistance. The feeling of excitement seemed to grow as Cain began to delight himself within the pleasures of his thoughts. Cain rejoiced over his father's reception at finding their home entirely remodeled and made anew.

These thoughts and more poured joy back into the hearts and spirits of both mother and child. Together the two worked tirelessly running back and forth to gather the sticky moss and collect syrupy dew. When maple and moss were no longer available as options the two resorted to using beeswax, and warm dung to help plaster the heavier coats. The sun that hung high in the sky was beginning to recede over the horizon. Its position indicated to the pair that they would need increase their efforts if they wanted complete their project in time. "Mother," Cain called out in alarm. "Father is sure to be home soon, we need to move quickly." His mother could only smile back at the boy and offer him a gentle nod signifying understanding and compliance.

Watching Cain as he darted and dashed back and forth to assist his mother was a warm sentiment that brought feelings of joy, and bliss.

Cain's mother looked on at him with bursting pride witnessing with objective lenses how well Cain was developing. The intimate moment filled the creature with a touch of sadness in coming to terms with Cains maturation and growth. It was if seeing Cain for the first time since his birth. He demonstrated exceptional skills and ability at assisting and supporting his mother. The nurturing experience would help to develop and later enhance Cain's character and confidence. His mother now looked differently at the young boy who seemed to be transitioning into a young man.

In the short time remaining the duo were able to complete the remarkable task of remodeling their home. When finally done the two stopped to look around at the toils of their labor and hard work. It was astonishing to see how much fuller and homely the cave now looked and felt. The cave was aesthetically pleasing to the eyes offering a tapestry of comfortable space perfect for relaxation. The bland walls of the cavern den no longer resembled that of a stony tomb but was now made lively and more homely. Additional layers of mane and hide were used decoratively like slip covers placed over boulders and other dense objects. Cain and his mother stood together looking over the beautiful canvas of their dwelling. The caved den appeared newly restored and immaculately radiant in their eyes. The use of different textures and patterns flushed against the siding and walls like wallpaper. The decorative backdrop contained the fur and skins of various creatures which surprisingly meshed well together.

The home improvement included the addition of a soft matted cot. Layers of heavy mane were stripped and cut from the hide and backs of lofty beasts to create a bed spread. Cain tarred and plucked away the feathers off the winged creatures. He collected the feathers and stuffed them into leathery sacks to create what Cain described as pillows. The remaining layer of fur and mane were elaborately placed over the ground to form a colorful tapestry at the center of the den. The strange combination of earthy colors was mostly unconventional however, the mash up of different tones and hues helped to brighten up the home and offset the plunder of darkness that once thrived. It was safe to say that the remodeling of their cavern transformed the bleak and somber dwelling into a comfortable living space. The caved den was substantially lofty in size however the two worked desperately to fill the room with decorations and accents as needed.

They used the large boulders strategically to model decorative furniture and table like placements around the cave. Plates and stones were arranged and placed on the base of spacious flat that would become the families dining area. The appeared was nearly complete as the two attended to a few minor and last-minute details. Mother and son worked tirelessly and finished just in time as the orange glow of the sun began to set removing daylight. "Where is father," Cain asked appearing somewhat worried and impatient. "Why has father not returned?" Cain looked to his mother for an explanation but found his mother unable to provide him with a reasonable resolve. Left without many options Cain planted his tired body down on the edge of the newly crafted bed and instantly found himself overcome with exhaustion and fatigue.

Cain could be seen stewing in his emotions fighting off the lingering symptoms of tiredness that was slowly creeping over him. He fought away the urge to yawn but was spotted a few times nodding off. Despite his strong will and determination Cain was no match against his weariness of his fatigued disposition. Cain wanted to be the first one to catch the first glimpse of his father's reaction to the surprise. He wished to be awake to see the look on his father's face as he walked through the doorway to witness first-hand the depth and extent of his family regard and appreciation for him. Unfortunately, Cain would miss the opportunity as the boys' eyes began to swell beneath the weight of his tired brows. Cain fought back against the temptation but found that he was not able to accomplish the feat of staying awake. It would be Ironic that Cain would fall asleep on the very cot and bed which he helped to design and build. The soft and rather comfortable setting seemed to betray Cains rogue intentions of staying awake. He appeared defenseless in his struggle to thwart away rest and sleep against his better judgment.

The sun had long since passed taking with it the remains of daylight however, Adam had not returned home. Cain had fallen asleep on the soft new bedding tired and exhausted from waiting on his father's arrival. Fear, and worry began to fill the heart and mind of Adams restless companion. The creature was unable to lay down or rest comfortably. The home renovations were truly impressive making for a comfortable and restful suite. However, his mate was unable to rest nor shake the jaded feelings of concern and worry that plagued the creature's heart and mind. These unsettling thoughts helped only to dull the creatures mind against the warrant and appeal for rest and recovery. Adam's mate refused the notion of sleep and instead began to pace back and forth through the cavern. The rhythmic sounds of pattering feet beating against the soft ground became somewhat of a melodic and soothing sound for the creature.

It wasn't long before after that the weary creature heard a strange sound coming from outside their home and doorway. It seemed as if something or someone was nearby. A shadowy figure seemed to be loitering outside the home. A loud and sudden groan filled the cave which instantly spooked and frightened the defenseless mother. The unknown invader appeared suddenly a massively tall creature engorged with bulk and girth. Adam's partner was frightened and overcome with fear and terror. The intruder seemed lost and somewhat misplaced stepping cautiously forward to better survey the canvas of the strangely decorated room. Retreating backwards Adam's mate stepped further into the cave disappearing behind the veil of darkness. The timid creature though fearful, and frightened was determined to protect its young from terrifying grips of the savage invader. His mate searched frantically in the dark for one of Adam's tools and managed to secure a blunt object that resembled that of a club. Adam's partner was prepared to defend their home and would use physical force to strike the intruder down.

Adam's mate began shaking uncontrollably overcome by fear and nervousness. This was a most unusual experience for Adam's partner who had grown routinely accustomed to living a mundane and peaceful life. However, this night it appeared that fate would refuse Adam's partner the grace of good fortune by removing peace and tranquility from their home. The climactic scene appeared dangerously nerve wrecking for Adam's mate who was now trembling with fear. The frightened creature heart thumped and pounded with nervousness each beat growing louder and grow more intense with every breath.

Adams mate was consumed with terror and very soon became convinced that the thumps were being amplified throughout the silent room. This strange delusion caused the creatures trembling nerves to become jittery and unmanageable. The sound of heavy breathing and chattering teeth quickly drew the intruder's attention to the direction of where Adam mate was presently hiding. The invaders keen and sharp eyed spotted the frightened figure of Adams mate standing deep within the bowels of the room shaking fearfully. An irrational sense of desperation gripped the frightened creature responding dramatically by releasing the club and covering its mouth. The sound of the club dropping confirmed the intruders' suspicions that someone was nearby. The noisy chatter of clashing teeth was no longer the creature's biggest problem as it was now much too late for Adam's mate as the savage invader having already caught sight and scent of the defenseless victim began to close in. Strangely the intruder moved sluggishly through the room as if dragging about the dead weight of its own body. Adam's mate observed the creature's sluggish trajectory and attempted to evade the intruder by slowly pivoting and stepping away. Adams partner searched to secure another instrument hoping this time for a much fiercer tool. It was too late it seemed the intruder began drawing closer into the home. Gripped by panic and fear the mute creature attempted frantically to cry out while pleading desperately for mercy and help.

The growing suspense of fear and terror was only rivaled by the tension of impending doom and fear in the room. Cain awoke suddenly stirred from his sleep by the sound of strange noises. Despite having obtained rest Cain appeared rather annoyed and somewhat irritated by the absence of his parents. Looking around Cains voice cried out suddenly in a happy and rejoicing toe. "Father!" Cain cried out jumping up quickly onto his feet to run and greet his father. Adam's mate stopped and peering in closer at the shadowy figure moving further noticed the resemblance that confirmed it was indeed Adam cloaked beneath a thick layer of mud and heavy debris. Adam managed to somehow get himself hurt while out in the fields. He had sustained a wounding injury that prolonged his return home. He hauled over on his shoulders a largely massive and monstrous beast whose long claws, and sharp horns offered plausible explanation to Adams current state and condition. Adam dropped the large creature off his shoulders and almost lost his balance and footing in the process nearly tumbling over and falling alongside his prey.

Removing the weight of the monstrous carcass Adam appeared relieved as he moaned painfully clutching to his sides. Cain was frightened and confused fraught with tears at the sight of his battered hero. He felt gripped with fear at never having witnessed his father so badly bruised beyond recognition. And even in his crippling condition Adam appeared unfazed smiling down happily at his son all while clutching hold of his midsection. "You will never guess what I brought home," Adam riddled in playful banter attempting to deflect from the dire gravity of the current situation. "I managed to take down a big one." Adam celebrated reaching down to pull the large creature's body up to present and display but stopped short after experiencing sharp throbbing pain in his side.

Adam condition appeared critical as his family sprang into action to offer him support. Cain and his mother moved quickly to aide Adam and were able to help him onto his knees before laying his body gently down on the floor. Working together once again mother and son struggled to carry the weight and load of Adam's body over to the soft comfortable bed. The two began a thorough and diligent search scouring over Adam's body in search of the wounded area. Adam had several cuts, scrapes and bruises which covered his body. They uncovered a deep gash and puncture on the left side of his lower abdomen that was bleeding out profusely.

Adam looked as though he had been repeatedly mishandled possibly tossed and heaved smeared through the dirt. Cain watched helplessly as his mother tended to his father's injuries. Adam could be observed drawing further away from consciousness because of the hemorrhaging wound. Cain fathomed in his mind a most fierce and epic battle waged, one that concluded with a near death and almost fatal experience for his father. The traumatic event caused a nuance of mixed feelings to develop within Cain. He was now upset and somewhat irritated by the senseless acts of violence, while simultaneously harboring feelings of delight and excitement at his father's unwavering victory. It was without a doubt that the young boy was eager if not looking forward to hearing the epic tale of the deadly encounter.

The punctured wound continued to slowly seep out draining Adams of life force. Blood ran down Adam's back like spewing water from of a punctured vase. Repulsed by sight of blood Adam's mates gagged instantly and nearly turned away however stopped and turned back with the understanding that Adam condition was dire and that he was in desperate need medical attention. If left unaided Adam would surely perish. His mate was urged by the call of their son who begged his mother to act. "Mother please do something." Cain pleaded crying hysterically. The creature acted quickly moving Adam hands from his sides and placing them over the wound and pressing tightly. Adam gave out a painful moan that served as an indication that he was still vaguely alert and oriented. Cain ran quickly to fetch his father water and returned with rags and shredded materials in his other hand. Together they tilted Adam over on his side to place rags over the moistened wounds.

Adam's mate applied pressure to the wounds using shreds of cloths that helped to cover the area, however, did very little to contain or stop the flow of blood. The shreds of cloths were beginning to feel damp and filled with moisture. Adam's mate become more anxious and fearful; the creature felt acutely attuned to the sensitivity of lapsing time. Adam partner appeared distraught and desperate ultimately at wits ends. The creature was left with very little options remaining to help keep Adam alive. Refusing to surrender and give up. Adam's mate sprang up and ran quickly to the newly furnished living space to secure more shredding. The creature tore away much of the decorated furnishing which covered their home. In doing so Adams mate was able to fashion a temporary gauze to wrap around the wounded area. The slack from the long strips of mane and hide were enough to cover Adam's abdomen and midsection. Adam's mates' technique though strange and unorthodox was useful in containing the endless flow of blood. Cain suggested out fear and desperation that they add another layer of wrapping to ensure that the wound would not reopen. However, his mother declined insisting that two layers were enough as the leathery hides were thick, and that an addition would only cause Adam further tension and discomfort.

The irony of the situation was undeniably remarkable what some would come to gather as fate. Nearly a decade had passed since the near fatal experience of childbirth that nearly claimed his lover and mate. Adam recalled how feverishly he toiled to help revive and restore his partners health all the while keeping death at bay. It seemed poetically justifiable that the very creature with whom Adam helped to rescue and save, was now bestowing grace and good fortune back over to him by returning the favor of rescuing and saving his life. The near fatal accident was helpful in bringing the couple closer together. The brush with death brought back lost and forgotten feelings of gratitude and appreciation which had been absent and longing between the couple. The nearly fatal experience engraved in their hearts a mutual respect and admiration for one another. They shared the same beneficial interests in ensuring the survival preservation of their family.

Adam and his mate were identical like two halves of a rare and priceless jewel. Each shard though rare with redeeming high quality and valuable in their appraisal. However, when presented fully formed and intact the exceptional jewel instantly becomes invaluable. That night the family slept plastered together between layers of soft and cushiony bedding. Adam found himself wedged comfortably between his endearing son and his loving companion. At home in bed with his family was preferably the safest resting place for Adam to heal and recover. It was true that the decoratively lounging area helped to provide the family a relaxing and comfortable space to gather. And though it was not the founder's intention, the comfortable area overtime began to take on the appearance of a medical detention center. Adam was not entirely enthused at the thought of being looked after like an infant or child. He would often exaggerate to his family the status the progress of his recovery of his health. However, he was unable to demonstrate his progress, nor could he move or sit up for long periods. Under the watchful eye and supervision of his family Adam was encouraged to remain on bedrest long enough to allow for his body to fully recuperate.

5

The Bonding

Several weeks had gone and passed by since the nearly fatal accident resulting in Adams injury. Though severely sore and bruised Adam was optimistic and hopeful of his recovery. He appeared to be slowly returning to good health, and regularly thanked his mate and child for helping to aide in his recovery. The warm sultry days of summer were beginning to come to a transitional end. The conventional change of the seasons welcomed the passive arrival of the fall season slowly ushering in the brisk autumn air. Adam had been inactive for some time. His body was noticeably frail and delicate since sustaining the injury. He now spent most of her days confined in the vicinity of his home. Adam seldom moved around never venturing beyond the borders of his doorway. He was not entirely immobilized however he was unable to walk long distances without calling out for rest whenever daunted by the task.

Fortunate for the family the beast that caused Adam's injury was large enough to sustain them for some time. The near-death experience had a strange effect over Adam impacting his behavior. He was noticeably withdrawn and recluse no longer finding interest in the hobbies of his pastimes. He no longer ventured outdoors for sport or attempted to hunt for strange and wild game. Instead, Adam took to the simple pleasures of life discovering new and less dangerous forms of activities. His daily routine included mostly sleeping and relaxing with intermittent breaks to allow for meal and consumption. He regularly extended his mid-day naps, often awakening in the evening just in time to pester and annoy his family with incessant whining and acts of neediness.

The newly found freedom and change of lifestyle afforded Adam the luxury of lying around his home in bed. Some days when able Adam would sit outside to bask beneath the warmth of the yellow sun. When the hobby of counting clouds became lifeless and boring Adam decided he would devote his time and energy to teaching his son the skill and art of hunting. His injury had dampened his attitude towards gaming however it did not remove the fact that their food supply and rations were beginning to dwindle. Adam's ability to provide and sustain his family's welfare was becoming more questionable. He was aware that he would need to return to the field; back to the hunting grounds to ensure his families wellbeing and survival.

Adam intended to teach Cain the jewels and gems to becoming a proficient hunter. "If I can train Cain to harness and holm his hunting skills he may possibly surpass and excel myself at having started training at such a tender age. "The delightful thought brought joy to Adam as he imagined Cain as a fierce warrior capable of hunting and bringing down fierce savages and beasts ten times his size. Adam relished over the thought of seeing his son as an adult standing proudly over his formidable opponent. The image of some strange beast having been conquered and subdued by the likes of Cain brought excitement and joy to the proud father. Returning to lucidity from the depths of his daydream Adam felt inspired to act and immediately went forth to fetch his son.

Adam found Cain in the company and presence of his mother with whom he spent most of his time. He engaged his mate and child providing a lengthy dialogue and detailed explanation as to the prevalent problem of their food shortage. It did not take much convincing or persuading from Adam finding his partner overly receptive and agreeable to the happy hand off. Cain was very much enthused and excited by his father's courteous offer to teach him how to hunt. A look of joy and enthusiasm could be observed drawn over Cains young face. He began to consider the epic odyssey of tales that his father had shared with him as a child.

Cain was now questioning whether he would be able to protect his father in the face of danger. A personal inventory of speculating thoughts, mostly filled by self-doubt and defeat corralled his young mind. The negative thoughts were intrusive highly fixated on the possible outcomes which may or may not occur. Cain knew for certain that he should not speak out loud or make his father aware of these uncertainties and insecurities. Cain looked up his father pacing steps ahead moving with a wounded stride. His swag was incomparable despite of his injurious condition. Cain was humbled thinking as to how he would be able to compare and measure up to that of his idol.

Adam was accustomed to traveling alone however today his son accompanied him. It was a most glorious day for the pair as they walked onward. They shared many thoughts, during the walk and touched on current events as well as other mature subjects. Adam found a new respect for his son; he had underestimated the depth and breadth of the young child's mind. Enraptured in this moment was the tender first bond between father and son. Today the two would hunt together joining forces in search of game and provisions.

Cain carried over his shoulders a large tote containing his father's many chiseled tools. Adams injury forced the hunters to keep a lame and sluggish pace resembling that of a precarious creature. The new garments which they wore thick leathery hides serving as padded layers of protections that were subsequently fashioned and adorned and laced with fur. These garments which were crafted and designed by the hands of his mate who insisted on protecting Adam, and most importantly the young child Cain from the dangers of the wild and untamed outback.

Adam did not like the idea of having to wear clunky clothing and swore against the ridiculous outfits. However, he but did not dispute its utility as his beloved mate insisted and ultimately refused to let their child charter the unknown regions without the added protection. Adam was unable to dispute or argue against logical reasoning for the need and use of protective layering. The implication that if Adam had been wearing padded garments the outcome of his injury could have been averted. Adam did not want to challenge his mate, nor did he want to prolong the tedious disagreement. He submitted willingly by throwing his arms into the air to be fitted and tailored. Draped in the latest warrior fashion the two were now clothed and ready to venture out into wilderness. Adam's and Cain's new clothes were tailored well, and made with quality materials sturdy, and thick. Inspired with care and safety in mind the garments served as deterrent barrier to avoid any possible accidents.

The growing bond between father and son was apparent and easily observed through their interaction. The thought of exploration brought Cain much joy but more so was the act of walking alongside his father. Despite the circumstances of Adams injury and limitations he still managed to teach his son a few life skills; sharing personal tricks and tactics for capturing wild game. Together the two chased and charged at the wild creatures and at other times found themselves retreating to avoid being trampled or even worse killed. Adam showed his son the land while mapping various sites, and locations in their discovery. Cain saw the feeding grounds where the creatures met to fight, and feast. "Do you see how the smaller wild beasts run from the larger wild beasts." Adam counseled his son observing the natural pecking of order of the land. The two hunters managed to find a vantage point overlooking the land in full view of the savage predators. Together they studied the behaviors of the beasts hoping to learn and further understand the social dynamics and norms of the savage inhabitants.

Cain was astonished to find such creatures roaming freely amongst them. "Amazing," remarked Cain marveling over the rouge cast of unsightly creatures. "The creatures are truly wonderful," Cain rejoiced with fascination. "Is it possible that we could somehow get a closer view?" Cain seemed more mesmerized than repulsed by the monstrous beast before him. "Father?' Cain called out, "where do all these creatures come from?" Inquired the young boy. Adam was stuck somewhat caught off guard by the unexpected line of questioning. He paused for a moment to search for council in his thoughts.

Looking down at the face of his son; it instantly dawned on Adam how quickly his son was growing. Adam projected himself into a space of empathy recalling on his own personal experiences at a similar stage of young life. Looking into the face of his son Adam began to envision and see a reflection of his younger self readily approaching the tender age of adolescence. Adam remembered the confusion, and the anguish that he felt from not knowing and not having answers to the questions which beckoned and gnawed at him incessantly.

Adam struggled internally with his conscious, "how, can I keep such a secret" he argued, "it is naive of me to believe that I could hide and shelter him from the world, believing as though he would never trail or travel the world discovering all that is beyond our home." Despite his painful injury Adam managed to stand up straight well enough to directly meet the brows and pupils of his son. "My father did..." Adam paused to correct himself, "I mean God created those creatures." "God?" repeated Cain seeming unsure, "your father, wait I do not understand."

"Who is God?" asked Cain with a discerning look of uncertainty and confusion on his face. His soft eyes widened patiently waiting for an answer and response to his inquiry. Adam hesitated for a moment seeming almost remorseful for his disclosure and considered for brief second as to whether Cain was ready to bare the truth of their existence. Adam pondered heavily on the gravity of his son's question, before finally deciding to share his light. "My son, God is the architect and creator of everything that you see before you." Adam paused briefly to allow Cain's mind a short moment to digest the meat and meaning of the loaded statement. Adam was careful to ensure his words were primed and well portioned to serve as food for thought. Cain looked even more confused as though unable to process the explanation that everything and everyone he saw before him was fashioned and sculpted by a sole artist and master creator.

"But how is that possible?" asked the inquisitive lad posing questions in search of clairvoyance. "How can one person create everything that lies before us?" "Did he create the sky?" quizzed the boy, "the moon, the sun, and what about the stars?" Adam accepted his son skepticism seeing as Cain was unacquainted with lineage and legacy of his grandfather. The idea of an omnipotent and mighty creator serving as ruler of all things existing was unimageable. The revelation appeared complex and somewhat unfathomable concept for a developing child to accept let alone conceive. "The answer is yes." Adam replied calmly to his son, "God created it all." He hopped that providing a definitive answer would bring a conclusion to the thread of inquisitions. Unfortunately, this was not the case as Adam found himself bombarded with follow up questions pertaining to the great creator. "Did God create the rivers... and the dirt... and the mountains too...." The questions came one by one like marching ants to from brigade of senseless thoughts. But before Cain could continue Adam stopped the boy mid-sentence.

"I see, the time has come," Adam said, to his small pupil, "It is time I tell you the story of how we all came to be." Adam searched the outskirts for shade and relief but only found large rocks and stones. Despite the uncomfortable jaggedness of the rocks Adam managed to secure a comfortable place to sit. Cain followed his father and was fortunate to find a seat beside his hero. The dense rocks provided shade from the scouring sun as well retaining an advantageous view of the hunting grounds. Cain crossed his legs and rested his chin into his palms. He had never heard stories this early in the day especially told in unfamiliar setting and territory. "In the beginning..." Adam began his oration speaking openly to his attentive son. The story lasted for some time, but Cain hardly noticed finding himself becoming engrossed in the tale. It was safe to assume that the duo would not find any game that day, having succumb to joyful distraction of storytelling. It went without saying that Adam and Cain did not spend most of the day searching for prey.

They would return home as they had left with nearly nothing to show for the day's work. However, this time neither Adam, or Cain appeared vexed by the situation or outcome. On the contrary Adam seemed pleased at having strengthen his connection and bond with his son. Cain also looked pleased if not ecstatic after discovering and learning of his royal lineage and history. Discovering his place as the rightful decedent of the first man was a great honor for Cain. The surprising news and discovery of God evoked a sense of pride within Cains heart and mind. He garnered delight in learning of his family's origin and acknowledging his direct connection and relation to the secular and sacred world. This idea and more seemed to excite Cain who was open to the thought of extended family which was a refreshing and welcoming thought.

The unsettling notion of his existence being merely coincidental, or simply an accidental occurrence was now erased. Exposed to the truth of his noble existence Cain now determined to declare his rightful place and position in the world. This great understanding seemed to offer the young boy great relief restoring and possibly rejuvenating his sense of spirituality and faith. Cain was fully immersed in the collective consciousness and belief that everything, and every creature was designed with intention and purpose and not by the act of blunder or chance. Cain no longer saw the world as an anomaly but rather he framed the universe as being a delicate piece of work. The world was now a masterpiece having been crafted and drawn out by an omnipotent and mighty ruler who was beyond all comprehension.

Father and son embarked on a lifelong voyage that would forever secure their bond and relationship. The connections made during the precious interaction between father and son would become sacred. The bonds they created on this day would sustain them for much longer than any morsel of meat ever could. The foundation that bridged and connected Adam with his son was cemented on this day. Cain looked up at his father and offered his shoulder as a crutch for Adam to lean against and walk. Adam accepted the warm gesture and wrapped his arm around his son's shoulder shifting most of his weight onto the youthful lad. "Father," Cain politely began as they walked home. "Yes," answered Adam, "Can you tell me again about the beautiful garden."

6

The Pilgrimage

Adam, and his son began to go out hunting more regularly. They enjoy each other's company and were happy working together as team. Adam taught his son the art of scavenging as well as how to track and stalk prey. Cain was burdened with responsibility of lugging around and carrying his father's tools. The upkeep of his father's tools was vitally important and necessary to ensure their survival. The sharp useful tools served purposeful in taking down prey and deterring against danger. Together their skills increased over time with each owning their own special technique and skill at hunting. Adam and Cain shared a natural inclination which helped them to become proficient hunters. Cain's abilities developed rather quickly as his imagination and keen intellect would become his greatest asset. Overtime Cain would become consumed with the need to improve his skills as hunter. He began to grow overly obsessed and fixated with improving his already impressive and rather fearsome hunting kills.

Cain wielded access to Adam's tools and cutlery collection however, he viewed his father's tools as prehistoric, and outdated. He came to accept that he would never come to harness the relic aged tools as diligently or skillfully as his father. It was these ideas, and more that ultimately led Cain to design and create his very own set of tools. Cain labored and toiled relying very much on his own ingenuity. The young man drew success and managed to craft two formidable tools which he presented to his father. The first tool in which he forged was a bow and arrow. The object as Cain described, "could be used to sphere a mark or prey from long and far off distances." The second tool was a leather sling which Cain presented equipped with a sack carrying marble, rocks, and small stones. "When flung with precision and strength this powerful tool can strike down a target with deadly force and accuracy." Cain placed a stone into the sack as he prepared to demonstrate the efficiency of his new design. "If used correctly the blunt impact of the stone will be enough to disable any prey or predator within range." Cain twirled the sling over his head to draw momentum before thrusting his arm forward to release the stone. The swift action sent the stone flying into the air soaring yards into the distance.

Adam was mesmerized by his son's ingenuity and was especially impressed with the sling. He recalled the strenuous and daunting task of having to forcefully heave and fling rocks with his hands. "This "sling" as you call it, will make hunting much easier." Adam rejoiced. He however disliked the bow and arrow declaring it impossible to use. Cains attempted several times to demonstrate the proper handling of the tool. However, Adam was inept and could not wield the item properly. He eventually became irritated referring to the tool, as "an abominable contraption." Cain was proud of his newly crafted tools which he came to call and refer to as "weapons". These weapons held endless possibilities for Cain as he looked to avoid close combat and preferred to keep distance and space between him and the target. Adam on the other hand preferred the method of close engagement finding utility and value in ensnaring traps. The two often disputed and debated over which hunting technique and strategy was most effective They politicized and philosophized back and forth between style, form and technique. Together the odd pairings were fairly matched against the distraught powers of the unknown and vast frontier.

Meanwhile on the other side of the land Tree was beginning to be grow lonesome. She worried about her friend. "I hope all is well with Adam for I have not seen him for quite some time." Unbeknown to Tree at the time Adam was contemplating the very same thought. One day while out with his son, Adam decided he would pay his close friend a visit. "Tree drew delight and joy in seeing Adam however she would rejoice more so after meeting Cain." A visit had been long overdue, it had been quite some time since Tree had laid eyes on the young prince.

One hot afternoon as the dry vibrant colors of autumn leaves lay across the dusty plains. A heavy gust of wind blew lifting the leaves off the ground and into the air. Tree watched as the leaves twirled and spiraled upward; dancing circles through the air before swaying back down to the floor. Tree found entertainment in watching the delicate dance of fanciful leaves. She loved watching the leaves move gracefully through the air. "Light and free," Tree thought to herself. "A single leaf has the potential to soar the sky and see the world depending on the touring winds and hasty current." These thoughts and more occupied Tree's thoughts and mind grounding her spirit in peace and serenity.

Tree diverted her attention momentarily after spotting two distant figures moving slowly in her direction. As the figures drew near Tree strained her eyes to make out a clearer image of the shadowy characters. After the creatures had walked some distant, she quickly recognized one of the adorned figures as her beloved Adam. Tree rejoiced gleefully crying out in excitement. She gasped immediately upon recognizing the distinctively tailored creature that accompanied Adam. The lengthy pilgrimage to visit Tree served as an act of homage. The expense of the tribute was paid through laboring steps and drenching sweat to meet their dear matriarch and honor her presence.

"Oh my God!" Tree, shouted out in a loud excited tone unable to contain her enthusiasm. "Adam!" She called out to him. "My dear friend, I thought you had forgotten me. It has been so long since I last saw you. It has been much too long since I last set eye on your face..." Adam wanted to rebuttal and provide a valid response but found no opportunity do so. Tree seemed overly enthusiastic by Adams visit and was unable to hold back or control her excitement. Tree could not believe her eyes. "Lo and behold," she went on, "I see you have brought with you a special visitor." "Hello, young man" Tree greeted the young boy.

"You must be Cain. The shy boy did not speak but rather looked on in silent amazement.

It was not so much Cains coyness which kept him silent but rather the astonishment and surprise of meeting a talking tree, "The creature knows my name." Cain answered shockingly "But how?" He searched his father's face for an answer but only found Adam wearing a playful smirk. 'Come my child," Tree encouraged, "do not be afraid, I will not bite." She laughed out loud giving Adam a playful wink.

Adam glanced at Cain and gestured with a nod for the boy to go forth and greet Tree. Cain was nervous, and hesitated as he slowly stepped forward. He dropped his head averting his gaze in effort to avoid staring directly into the face of the grand sage. Adam saw this and placed his hand gently beneath his son's chin, "Do not be afraid" Adam reassured his son, "Tree is part of our family. She is my closest, and dearest friend. She only wishes to meet you and has not seen you since you were a small child. Show her how much you have grown she will not hurt you." The timid young boy stepped forward and slowly raised his head up to meet the face of Tree.

"Hello Cain," Tree announced, "how are you today young prince?" Cain was still uncomfortable with the thought of a talking tree. He nodded and agreed with a nervous smile struggling to communicate or provide a dignified response. His eyes were fixed on Tree looking over the gigantic tree with sheer astonishment and amazement. He examined her body closely with his eyes and scratched his head as if still uncertain. Cain pondered as to the sort of magic and sorcery that allowed and granted Tree the voice and ability of speech. Adam swooped Cain into his arms and lifting him onto his shoulders he brought his son closer to Tree's high limbs. "Let me get a good look at you," Tree requested glowing joyfully, Cain was nervous and somewhat uncomfortable with being perched high up. He reacted instinctively by clinging desperately to Tree's branches and limbs.

The high altitude caused an alarming frenzy of wails and outcry from young boy pleading hysterically. His hands and small fingers plastered tightly across Tree's face in somewhat of a terrified embrace. Adam reached up to lift Cain off her shoulder setting him back down on the ground. Adam had barely placed Cain back on the floor when the young man pulled away jumping out of Adams arms and onto his feet. Cain took off in a playful sprint running circles around Tree and Adam begging to be chased. "Catch me father" Cain shouted darting back and forth circling the two adults. Tree drew amusement at the agility of the young child and was more so impressed by the quickness of Adams feet trailing closely behind his son.

Tree marveled at their playfulness of the pair and cheered on both runners as they dashed about. She laughed loudly at the entire spectacle and would have continued laughing had it not been for a small fruit that struck against the backside of her head. Searching around for the culprit Tree was unable to tell in which direction that the fruit was hurled. A nagging suspicion crept over Tree as she heard the whimsical sound of laughter echoing behind her. She did not need a second set of eyes to see that it was Adams playfully mischievous son Cain who was now laughing as he flung more fruits into the air.

Without hesitation or reprieve Tree gave out a playfully loud war cry in response to the assault. Adam responded to the pouring outcry by moving swiftly to Tree's defense. He emerged suddenly at her side shielding himself behind Tree's robust figure and build to escape the onslaught of flying fruits. "No," Tree laughed, "do not hide behind me..." Just then a piece of fruit crashed across the side of Tree's face which quickly ended their horseplay. Cain felt terribly remorseful fearing he had overly extended beyond the boundaries of playfulness. Adam too stopped, understanding they had taken their buffoonery too far. The two shot glances back and forth at each other in confusion before calling for cease fire. "Tree!" Adam cried out, "Tree are you alright?"

Tree did not respond but kept her eyes closed and tightly pressed. She was unable to see the look of remorse and worry on the small child's face. "Get him!" Tree suddenly cried out playfully deploying Adam to follow up against her attacker. "Grab that boy and bring him here to me." Tree summoned with jovial laugher. Despite Trees encouragement, Adam was much too clumsy. He lacked the grace and endurance needed to qualify for Tree's minion-ship. Adam failed miserably in his attempts and efforts to capture the elusive child.

Adam felt equipped and well-prepared wielding two small fruits in his hands. He jumped out suddenly from behind Tree, and quickly found himself stationed at the forefront of a battlefield. Adam would quickly learn that he was unmatched and ill prepared to set challenge against the thrust of his Cain's sling. The boy slung the fruits with precision, and spot on accuracy. Adam was stuck instantly by a plum that exploded upon impact colliding against his arm and chest. Before Adam could respond or cry out from the pain another fruit came hurling in his direction only this time it was a pear that would hit his foot. "Ahhh, my foot!" Adam cried out hopping around on one foot. The onslaught caused Adam to jump back and retreat helplessly behind Tree. Adam felt trapped, and somewhat entrenched as he was unable to draw away or escape without receiving a harsh blow to his legs and sides.

Tree from her scaling disposition owned an advantageous view of the rigid warzone. She took notice of Adam's disadvantage and decided to offer him some support. "Do not worry," Tree reassured Adam. "Help is on the way." Tree shook her bushy head, and down fell an arsenal of fruits dropping like hefty care packages onto the ground. Adam was amused by the display and rejoiced with laughter searching the floor for ammunition. He was fortunate to find several pieces of fruits at his disposal. Adam gathered as many fruits as he could managing to retrieve a cluster of fruits without being struck. Gazing over the artillery of ammunition, at his disposal Adam was careful in choosing only the softest fruits. He deliberately avoided dense hard fruits like apples and oranges. Fully stocked with ammunition of fruits at his disposal Adam was now ready if not prepared to engage his opponent in what appeared to be a gourmet combat.

Adam the war machine dove out from behind Tree into the open battlefield in a timeless motion quickly drawing and returning fire.

Adam chucked, and pitched several fruits in Cains direction, and managed with heightened sense of agility to catch and hurl back fruits in midair as they approached him. Cain drew excitement at going head-to-head against the greatest warrior he'd ever known. Adam reigned supreme in all faucets of sport and competitions however, the space and distance that separated the two contenders was gradually being diminished. It was difficult to distinguish the severity of the situation seeing as the contenders were unable to hold back the joyful sounds of laughter.

Cain was very agile moving rather quickly ducking and dodging attempting desperately to escape the attack of approaching fruits. "Ouch!" Cain cried out suddenly. He had been struck in temple by a fast-flying lemon that stunned the warrior and instantly disarmed the young man. Cain gave up the battle crying out in pain and attending to the swelling knot that was beginning to form on his head. He attempted to declare his surrender however, Adam was relentless and unmerciful in the competitive spirit and nature. He set after the young boy giving him chase. Cain harnessed agility and quickness as a fresh and vibrant youth, however Adam was primed with tenacity and determination.

The two ran circles around Tree. The playful display amused Tree, so much that she gave out a big bellowing laugh. She laughed out loud, and each time with more intensity than the last. "Go on Adam, you got him now!' she cheered out, "Get that little rascal." Adam mustered up all his energy in attempt to keep up traction and motion in his sprint. "Oh... my," thought Tree, "I haven't laughed like this in a very long time."

Adam was relentless, he trailed behind the small boy determined to catch and bring an end to the exhaustive amusement and play. Adam dove into the air after the child with a heaping leap forward. In the air his shadow covered the young boy, and for a moment it seemed Adam would have Cain pinned down. But the boy was intuitive and stopped short dashing quickly out of the way and narrowly escaping Adams grasp midair. Cain watched in slow motion as his father went flying over his head plummeting to the ground.

Adam fell and though he was unharmed his ego was now battered if not bruised by the unfortunate mishap. Tree who had witnessed the entire ordeal was helpless to refrain or hold back her laugher. Smiling at Adam as he walked back to her, Tree managed to offer Adam a few kind words of affirmation. "Good try son." Tree laughed out loudly, "you will surely get him next time." Looking over in direction of the energetic boy still running about playfully. "Is he, like this all the time?" Tree asked in her observation. "Yes," answered Adam still winded and out of breath. "But I never knew he could run so fast." "He reminds me of you when you were that age." Tree laughed recalling Adam's childish qualities and traits which he had since forgotten.

The two sat together to reminisce and catch up. Adam provided an update and accounting of all that had occurred and taken place since their last meeting. Adam explained how he came to wear such ridiculous garments, and proudly showed off the scar from his wound. Their reunion was a pleasurable sight to behold. The two shared jokes and laughed amongst one another recalling on historical and past events. Adam, and Tree ruminated for some time on many of the memorable moments, and experiences they shared together. Their interaction and engagement filled Adam with immeasurable bliss. The special moment helped to rekindle long-lost feelings within Adam that he believed had been extinguished.

The two friends talked for some time. Adam sat perched beneath the limbs of Tree's shaded branches. They sat watching over the young child as he played carefree amongst the windy leaves. Cain was fully enthralled in child play unaware of the peering sentinels who were monitoring and watching him from a distance. Adam rose suddenly to pick a fruit off Tree's bushy hair. He plucked his favorite fruit and sat back down to take a bite. Adam bit the fruit and chewed delicately with calming silence. Adam relished over the sweet tasting fruit which conjured feelings of nostalgia. Adam began to entertain in his mind the thought of abandoning his carnivorous diet and returning to his former regiment of natural organic foods.

Cain spotted Adam eating the fruit and looked rather perplexed and confused at his father. Adam appeared to be chewing away at the soft colorful rocks which they hurled back and forth at one another just moments before. Cain attempted to mimic his father by picking up a similar fruit he found lying on the floor. Cain would have bitten into the fallen fruit had it not been for Adam and Tree who yelled out to him and stopped him from taking the bite.

"No!" Adam screamed out to his son, "do not eat from the ground." Adam warned. "Come here and eat with us." Cain, walked over to his father, and glancing over the ground at the many fruits scattered before him. The thought had never dawned on the small boy that these shapely objects which he flung about freely were somehow delectable foods of some sorts which could be consumed or eaten. "Come closer" Adam called out to his son, "stand beside me." Cain moved closer in proximity as Adam pointed up into the direction of Tree's leafy green hair. "Look up and tell me son which fruit you would like to taste first." Cain slowly peeled his eyes away from his father and fixing his gaze upward he was surprised to discover a rare assortment of ripened and fresh fruits. Cains eyes began to widen marveling over the abundance of delicious fruits hanging over their heads.

Cain awed in amazement somewhat entranced by the pallet of wonderful colors that bloomed so tastefully and decoratively above him. "Go on." Tree encouraged observing Cains hesitation. "You are welcome to have more than one fruit if you choose." Adam offered Cain a bite from the fruit which the weary boy begrudgingly accepted. However, after tasting the juicy and rather supple fruit Cain found himself unable to resist the tasty morsel. He set into a frenzy motion and quickly move to consume the rest of the fruit directly from his father's hand.

Cain could hardly contain his excitement and pleasure and made little effort to conceal his desire to try more. "May I have another?" Cain politely requested, then shortly requesting for another, then another. The small boy begged to taste them all pointing away at different fruits. Ambitious in his goal Cain was very much determined to try ever fruit devouring the tasty fruits in three sometimes four consecutive bites. Cain went on for some time tasting the variation of fruits learning through the sensation and color. Cain learned effectively the sweet and bitter differences between various fruits. He experienced the tarty distinction between lemons and limes, apples and oranges peaches and pairs different variations of edible delights. Cain had become somewhat of a refined connoisseur of natural delectables.

Shortly after Cain had taken in his fill, he knelt positioning himself beside his father. His protruding belly demonstrated the outcome and effect of overindulging. Cain was now overcome with the urge to sleep. He had eaten to his hearts content and was now feeling the heavy weight of sleep draping over him. Cain yawned and stretched out his arms, nestled himself next to his father, and in a near instance fell fast asleep. Adam, and Tree hardly noticed for some time, until a strange humming sound caught both their attention. "It seems that our noble prince has set forth yet on another side quest." Tree announced rather playfully. "The triad's have somehow become dyad's," Tree laughed jokingly very amused by her own wit and playful banter. Adam quickly joined in the uproar until very soon the sound of laughter began to subside and die down. The joyous moment was immediately followed by an awkward linger of silence. Adam was in deep thought as his mind began to race and wander. Tree was unsure what to say to break the awkward tension and just as she prepared to speak, she was startled by bellowing sound of Adam's voice.

7

The Pilgrimage Cont.

"Tree, may I ask you, a question?" "Yes, why of course Adam." Tree, answered, "you can ask me anything you wish." He thanked her and slowly began to speak tenderly. "This child of mine, though I cherish him dearly he requires ample care and attention. Cain is a very peculiar creature who loiters throughout the day but will not sleep at night. He simply lays awake begging to hear endless stories while offering false if not empty promises to end his requests."

Tree bit her bottom lip in effort to remain subjectively unbiased in listening to Adam sharing his personal struggles and grief. "I offered to take him today so that his mother could have a peaceful moments rest..." Tree struggled to conceal her growing amusement and smile, she listened. She fought back against the swelling impulse to laugh out loud listening to Adam divulging his gripes and grievances with child rearing.

Adam took notice to the queer smirk on Tree's face but chose to ignore it. Her expression unsympathetically hinted at the direction of his complaints. Tree listened to Adam's list of concerns while thinking back to the early days of Adam youth and childhood. Tree was unable to draw any notable distinctions or differences between Cain and Adam during his youth and childhood. The description of Cains behavior was identical and mirrored that of Adam's behavior at his age. In her mind she giggled and smirked as Adam professed his grievances unfurling his anxieties. Tree suspected Adam's lingering premise would lead to the swelling question, the query in which Tree had already considered with foresight and anticipation. She intended to confirm Adam's suspicions by grading his behavior as more radical and misbehaved than Cain. Tree had already accepted the verifiable of truth and was prepared to respond to the unspoken question with an affirming and solid "yes!"

"...On other days" Adam continued, "Cain is as nimble and silent as the stoic winds however these quiet moments and instances are often rare." What I want to know Tree, is whether or not, this is normal behavior for a child." Adam swallowed his pride and prepared to share his thoughts. "Was I..." Adam began to inquire however stammered nervously over his words. He turned his attention to Tree who at the time appeared constipated with amusement. She sealed her and bit them so as not to smile or break out into laugher. "Would you say that growing up I was a..." but Adam could not complete his question.

"You are wondering," Tree interrupted, "whether you behaved like Cain at his age." Adam could not believe it, Tree, had ambushed his thoughts, and somehow read his mind. He smiled back with a degree of embarrassment drawn over his face. "Yes." Adam answered, "My childhood and youth was so very long ago and hard for me to recall." Adam began to explain, I can hardly imagine myself ever having been that small." He laughed compulsively, "Tell me Tree," Adam asked, "was I as misbehaved as Cain? At this age." Expecting to hear no, Adam, was surprised when Tree, gave out a giant bellow of laughter. "Oh yes, Adam you were terrible," Tree laughed out loud, "oh you were simply diabolical." Tree playfully joshed, "you were quite the menacing misfit in your youth." Adam responded with an equally bellowing sound laughter. "Do not fib Tree," Adam responded jokingly, "tell it truthfully, I was indeed quite the easygoing child." The two sat together for some time in good spirits, laughing and sharing intimately the joy of each other's company.

The sounds of their joyful laughter could be heard echoing through the air traveling far off in the distance. The purest of all sounds was the vibration of laughter which could be heard and felt as a frequency above the clouds reaching the realms of heaven. The wavering sounds of joy and laughter managed to attract the attention of one all-knowing and powerful entity. God watched over the entire engagement unfolding before him. God was witnessing first-hand the tenderness and love Adam exhibited towards his son.

In viewing the intimate display between the two beings God began to dwell on his own relationship with Adam possibly reconsidering some decisions that he made. The love and regard Cain held and reserved for his father did not go unnoticed. God observed the natural behavior and display of affection demonstrated by the small child. Cain displayed open admiration towards his father and creator. The relationship between Adam and Cain captured within the dynamic dichotomy the essence of his initial and intended plan. It was the purpose and reason for his initial creation of man, to love and honor him unconditionally.

God failed to consider the effort and length of time that it took Adam and Cain to form their cohesive bond. The requited love and regard that the two shared for one another was not formed during conception or contracted during creation. Adam and Cain forged and developed their relationship holding firm to the idea of family and solidarity. The strength of their bond was reinforced by Adams persistent commitment to his family. Adam chose to be present and active consistently aligned with the assigned roles of provider and protector of his home. God refused to consider the impact of his absence in Adams life neglecting the thought of never having shared the same affection and intimacy that Adam displayed towards his son. God watched on for as long as he could listening to the sound and melody of their laughter. It seemed that by sheer will and way of alchemy Adam had managed to successfully to transfer his legacy and life into lifeforce and being. More astonishing was the fact that he did so while still retaining honor and admiration through the eyes of his creation. "That is all ever I wanted," God whispered to himself, "nothing more." God had long ago given up on the idea of fulfilling his masterful plan. In his resentment he declared the creation of man to be a foiled and forsaken experiment which yielded unintended outcomes. However, in viewing Adam's interaction with Cain he began to reconsider his previous notion of vile dominancy he assigned to Adams dependents. Cain was ultimately God's descendent and natural kin to the king. He was first grandchild conceived without his consent despite the kings wishes. God reflected on his initial disapproval of the matter but now those very objections now seemed meaningless to him.

God appeared touched by the intimate gathering which brought him pleasure. He watched from above at the joyous reunion, observing the affectionate exchange between creation and creator. The love appeared identical to the tenderness that Tree reserved for Adam. This was truly a touching sight and moment to behold. God secretly wished that he could share in the joyful engagement however, he could not fathom the thought of making an appearance. He held the unshakable belief that his brash and sudden appearance would be unwelcoming and met with disdain. God imagined his reception would be met by scouring frowns and beaten brows irritated by his arrival. These distressing thoughts and more seemed to fill his mind as he replayed over the chaotic scene that was their last encounter and engagement. Very soon the king's eyes began to swell filling up slowly with tears. God considered the precipitating events that led to Adam's expulsion and removal from Eden. He commiserated over all that had transpired and taken place between the two and concluded that it was best that to avoid meddling in personal affairs.

God watched on from his celestial throne deeply moved however saddened, that he could not find a cause or reason to bring himself to join Adam, Tree and meet his grandchild Cain. The kings' eyes began to swell and soon tears began to run down his face as he wept piteously. The impact of the king's disappointment could be felt and heard on earth as bolstering sounds of thunderclaps. There was a sudden change in climate as thick clouds began cluster and consume the sky. God's tears passed seamlessly through the foundational floors of heaven to form large rainclouds. It was not long before trickles of raindrops began to shower over the dry and dusty earth.

Adam and Tree witnessed first-hand the sudden change in the weather. They observed the drastic shift and were somewhat baffled by the sudden transition. They looked on with discerning curiosity as though drawn to the sound of the rumbling sky and the clouds gathering before them. "What is happening? Adam pleaded openly, "I do not understand the skies were clear, but now look," stretching out his arm to feel the rain against his fingertips. "I do not know either," Tree joined in, "I do not understand the reason for such strange and sporadic weather." The rain began as light gentle taps pattering softly over the surface of the gentle ground. But as God continued his pouring outcry so would his tears continue to shower and pour down over the earth. What began as a gentle shower developed quickly into intense and forceful rainstorm drawing intensity and force.

The fierce sound of raindrops beating against the ground began to startle the young boy. Cain was unaccustomed to being outside in the rain and most often avoided the moist climate. He preferred to stay warm and dry within the confines of home. And often refused to leave the cave when confronted with possibility of precipitation and rain. However, in this instance Cain was nowhere near the dry cozy sanctuary of his dwelling and home. He clung nervously to his father's side standing beneath Tree's sturdy branches like an umbrella. Her thick boughs and leafy limbs helped to shelter Adam and Cain them from the pouring rain. "What is the matter my son," Adam asked looking down at Cain. "You tremble as though you are fearful or frightened by the sudden appearance of rain." Cain did not answer but clamored desperately to his father's side after being startled by thunderous booms and sounds of rolling clouds.

The frightened boy with tightly closed eyes burrowed his face into his father's shoulder as though trying disparately to avoid the whistling sound of howling winds. Adam appeared vexed if not upset by his son's reaction witnessing first-hand the manifestation of fear being formed.

Cain's nerve-racking reaction to the presence of thunder and fierce rain was rather unsettling. "Do not be afraid" Adam reassured his son, "of the howling winds, or the expanding clouds. Do not allow the booming sounds of the thunder to unnerve and frighten you. I have come to learn and discover these sounds often indicate the production of fresh rain-water. The rain cannot harm or hurt us my son." "Yes," confirmed Tree interjecting, "Do not let bad weather discourage or turn you away from venturing the uncharted world. If you can face adversity and not be frightened or overwhelmed by the challenge than you too will become brave like your father. Fearless and capable of navigating this world or anywhere that you may find yourself placed."

Adam was moved by the sentiments of Tree kind words. He placed his hand gently on Cain's shoulders and with his palms Adam wiped away the tears from his son's face. "Look up at the sky." Adam directed pointing up into the clouds. "You see son," Adam began to explain, "on our journey we will come across many challenging storms that will test us. These hardships and instances often difficult and challenging will present as fixed and immovable. However, nothing is permanent or stationary as they appear. Along my journey I have come to learn that discomfort is temporary and that nothing lasts forever. If you can learn to weather the difficult storms and hardships of life without being overwhelmed or torn down, then you will emerge each time wiser if not stronger than when you first encountered the storm."

Cain was comforted by his father words and slowly began to reclaim his courage and confidence from deep within. In a show of solidarity Cain unfastened a layer of his padded clothing and in removing the garment placed the leathery hide of support over his father's shoulder, "I believe that I can manage without it," Cain answered now holding the padding over his father's head. Adam was moved by his son's affectionate display of concern displayed towards him. In Adam's mind and heart, the sacred trinity was now fully complete. Peering into his son eyes he could see that his Cain was no longer a pubescent boy but rather an adolescent teetering towards adulthood.

"I will always protect you." Adam reminded his son, "Nor will I allow any harm to come your way." "And what about mother?" Cain teased playfully. "Yes," Adam answered definitively. "Your mother especially." "And what about Tree?" Cain posed rhetorically. "Yes, I will protect Tree as well." "And what about..." Cain attempted to host a list of rhetoric's, however Adam managed to interrupt the flood of rash inquiries by providing reassuring clarity to his son. "We are family Cain, and family takes care of one another." Adam concluded abruptly with a warm smile and a gentle pat on his head.

The crippling sound of loud thunder erupted from within the gray balls of clouds. The blaring explosion managed to disrupt what seem to be a precious and tender moment between father and son. Cain responded with a fright and reacted accordingly by releasing his grip and hold over the makeshift canopy. The result of the quick caused rainwater to fall and soak Adam's head. Another loud thunderclap cracked and ripped through the air. The thunderous noise served as a source of panic, and anxiety for Cain. The loud sounds only helped to derail his attention and concentration from Adam. Cain seemed uneasy in the moment having quickly lost the newly discovered sense of confidence and self-assurance just obtained. "Trust me," Adam reassured his son grabbing hold of Cain's hand and wrist. Cain was reluctant and resisted his father's pull but found himself being forcibly pulled out into the open rain.

Together the two slowly stepped out from beneath Tree's sheltering branches to brave the showery rainstorm. Cain shook nervously appearing frightened and rather uneasy with the entire undertaking. He looked as though he wanted desperately to cry out and jerked nervously but was unable to free himself from his father's grips. There was nowhere for him to escape. Adam could sense Cain's growing apprehension. He was becoming observably uneasy and tense in the matter. He squirmed and clawed frantically digging his sharp nails deep into Adams hands attempting to remove his fastened hold. When nothing else seem to prevail, Cain shut his eyes in an act of defiant surrender. He was ready to accept his fate and embrace the fierce storm of raindrops colliding against his body and running down his face.

The rainfall beat down hard over their heads drenching and soaking their bodies. The rain dampened their clothes causing the wet mane of supportive garments to sag and droop as a result. Cain felt a sense of safety and reassurance while in the presence of father. Having his father beside him served as a protective forcefield that helped to repel doubt and fear from entering his thoughts. The constant precipitation of rain that soaked Adam and Cain resembled that of a baptism with water raining down and over their heads. The symbolic gesture seemed to wash away the preconceived notions that Cain once reserved. He was in sense being cleansed from his baseless childish fears surrounding the dangers of the world. Cain blushed at his own ignorance, and feeling somewhat silly after overcoming his crippling fear of rainstorms. In retrospect Cain considered how silly and senseless the entire notion seemed. "I cannot imagine," Cain laughed with amusement, "that I was ever freighted by rainwater." As if suddenly surprised by the stunning revelation, he burst out with laughter and excitement. Witnessing his son's jovial reaction and temperament Adam decided to join in on the laughter. The two broke out in an improv of song and laughter both father and son celebrating carelessly while dancing in the rain. Cain was ecstatic most of all and demonstrated his excitement by prancing and frolicking in mitts of a sweltering rainstorm.

Cain was unmistakably happy and oozed with excitement feeling free if not liberated from the confines of his trepidation and fear. Somehow with the assistance and support of his father Cain managed confront and overcome one of his childhood fears. Cain threw his arm across his father's shoulders to offer a rejoicing and playful embrace. Adam stood in silent astonishment at his son. It was if Adam was seeing his son again for the first time. He took was very much impressed by his son's carefree attitude and free-spirited demeanor. These qualities and character traits seem to distinguish and set the two apart. Cain lifted his head up to face the sky and suddenly without cause, he began to berate and taunt the clouds. He was filled with excitement at having overcome and triumphed against a personal adversity. This was truly a joyous occasion for Tree as she watched Adam and Cain laughing and playing beneath the showering rainstorm. The two stomped and jumped on puddles of water splashing and splattering about carrying on like nonsensical children. Adam and Cain appeared unfazed by the soiling and dampening of their robes. Their mudded bodies and furry linens were now decorated and covered in mud and debris.

The joyous and tender moment was interrupted by Tree, who suggested to Adam, and his son that they should escape the rain, and seek refuge by returning home, "I think it best you venture home now," Tree encouraged, "it is for the best that you remove yourself from this unsavory climate and harsh weather." Adam was receptive to Tree's recommendation. "You are right." Adam agreed, "It is best that we retire and begin our travel home. Cain offered Tree a tender embrace and farewell.

"Goodbye Tree," announced Cain, "it was nice meeting, thank you for the wonderful bruits," "Your welcome sweetheart, and there called fruits," She quickly corrected the young boy. "You and your father are more than welcome to take some extra food back home with you," Tree shook her head causing more fruits to fall and drop down from her branches. Cain moved quickly to gather more fresh fruit before returning to his father's side wielding an armful of delectable fruits "I will have more fruits for you the next time you visit," Tree declared. "Thank you." Adam responded graciously. "We will be back to visit you again very soon my dearest friend." Adam relieved his son of the burden by offering to help Cain carry home some of his fruits. Goodbye Tree!" shouted Adam once more waving off into the distance. Cain wanted to mimic his father by waving goodbye, however, he was unwilling to risk or jeopardize dropping any of his delicious fruits. They began their descent home walking fearlessly defiant beneath the wrath and fury of a vengeful storm.

The Degradation

The fierce rainstorm began to wither and soften shortly after Adam and Cain's departure and return home. Tree found herself once more alone in the silent and peaceful company of her own thoughts; or so she liked to believe. It was at that moment and instance that God chose to appear before her. Tree had been resting her eyes and was unaware of her master's arrival. It was the acoustic sound of rain drops pattering against the ground which she found soothing. These sounds often helped to put her into a tranquil state of deep rest and sleep. This time however Tree was unable to rest or find peace. An eerie rather and rather powerful presence was preventing her from securing the rest she desired. The sunlight which illuminated the space shown more radiant than sun. It was safe to assume that being in the presence of the omnipotent king was difficult to ignore.

It would be nearly impossible for any creature to find sleep or rest while in the presence of the grand master and creator. Tree awoke somewhat irked and irritated by the brightness of the sun. However, she quickly gathered her composure after realizing that she was standing before her mighty king. "Oh, my lord..." she fumbled about while collecting her composure. "How are you?" God did not answer Tree, but instead offered a scouring look of repugnance. The pensive gaze he directed at Tree aligned perfectly with kings' mood. The fierce glare was reserved for the foulest and trattorias of traitors. Tree was confused by God's silence, and just as she was about to inquire and speak out the king took in a deep breath. Tree paused her thoughts expecting to hear a word from her king but instead God frustratingly exhaled a heavy heap of air from his flaring nostrils.

His dramatic animation captured Tree's attention causing her to grow uneasy. She held her breath in suspense awaiting his words. In a despairing tone he spoke, "Tree, today I watched you and Adam enjoying yourselves." "Oh, why yes, your highness," Tree responded abruptly "today was quite an eventful day..." But stopped, after seeing the look disdain drawn over her master's face. God was neither entertained, nor amused by her testimony. Tree quickly silenced her-self to allow her lord to continue with his thoughts. God began once again. "As entertaining as you may find the situation, I remain irritated at the fact that Adam has yet to return to me. He does not strike me as one who intends to bow before my feet. He remains unfazed and unwilling to repent or plead for my forgiveness or mercy. He has yet to make any offering to mend our severed relationship. It is safe to assume by his action that Adam has no desire or plan to pledge his loyalty or allegiance to me."

God fell awkwardly silent and withdrawn. A scorned look of repute and disgust was now drawn across his face. "I spared his life!" The king exclaimed, "showed him mercy when vengeance would have easily sufficed," God inhaled deeply through his nostrils a heavy gust of remorse, "Adam should have run back to me by now! God yelled, "Pleading, and begging for my mercy and for my forgiveness." Tree looked on at her king with growing sorrow and pity. "I do not understand it. "The king continued. "Why does Adam choose to mock me so by squandering his life away. He has chosen to become an undomiciled recluse living out here in the desolate wilderness. Adam could have easily pled for my mercy and grace and asked to be restored and returned home to the paradise that I created for him."

God exhaled a heavy breath of exhaustion from his lungs. "This was not the plan that I designed for my greatest creation." God professed, peering directly into Tree's face watching on with moistened eyes. "Expelling him from Eden was rash, and poorly calculated on my part. I did not intend for Adam's exile to extend beyond the duration of a few days. But when he did not call out to me, I became infuriated. I never imagined that pride and arrogance would corrupt my creation to the point that contempt and disregard would consume his identity." God unpacked his disappointment and frustration regarding Adam which left the air around them awkwardly silent and tense.

Tree felt somewhat confused and emotionally compromised by the complexity of her disposition. Tree was burdened internally somewhat conflicted the dueling roles and prevailing ideologies. At one end she had given and devoted her life's service to the being Adam's guardian and caretaker. On the other end she owed her allegiance and very existence to God. He was her master and creator rightfully the supreme king. "He mocks me!" God convinced himself. "He aims to make a fool of me!" Tree did not have an answer or a reply for God and remained silent in her wisdom. She was somewhat saddened by her inability to produce the correct combination of words to disarm her master from his troubles and anguish. Tree's complicit silence resonated in the mind and heart of the king. God expected Tree to jump to Adams defense however in the absence of her scrutiny and council the inaudible gesture appeared uncertain. It was difficult to discern whether Tree was protecting Adam from Gods unbridled wrath and fury or whether she was indifferent to the matter. The lingering notion did not go unnoticed by the king deliberating in his thoughts.

The moment of silence had stretched beyond comfortability slowly trailing into the realms of awkwardness. It was God who decided not to allow any dormant contentions or harbored feelings to sully his path or purpose. "I watch him." The king openly confessed, "obsessively more than I should have. Initially watching Adam struggle brought me great relief and entertainment. However, I soon became enthralled if not fascinated by his display of primal resiliency. My curiosity and growing interest led me to accidentally subscribe and monitor more frequently the days of Adam's life. For several seasons I observed the direction of plight of his progress and growth. I became a passively obsessed and began to watch him intrusively. From the time and instance that he emerges from his caved dwelling until he retires and re-turns home, I watched over him. I was present if not watching as Adam struggled to adjustment to the new environment around him. How-ever, he has learned to tread the unpaved foundations of the secluded bedrocks with impeccable mastery and skill." God appeared emotion-ally conflicted and torn. His eyes swelled with tears as he spoke open heartedly about his creation.

"I watched Adam on his first exploration," God disclosed, "as he chartered the foreign and unknow region. I saw first-hand the look of disbelief on his face when he placed his sights on those revolting and grotesque creatures settled around him." The words fell softly from the kings' lips as he hung his head in shame and disbelief . He spoke can-didly as if left alone with only his private thoughts. "Those monstrous creatures I banished were impure and defected deserving of damnation, and exile but not Adam..." God did not bother to look up at Tree as he spoke, he behaved rather evasively by avoiding her gaze and sympathy. Tree listened objectively without judgment as her king spilled out his heart. God had never openly discussed with Tree surrounding his trou-bles and grievances. Tree did not dare interrupt her king in such a pas-sion filled state. She instead offered her master a listening ear and only when requested would she provide and offer council.

"My greatest creation set aside, and caste away, forced to live amongst the most ratchet of beasts. I have stationed Adam in the most unfavor-able of conditions and circumstances. I did not intend for this to be-come his fate to live his days grazing the barren outskirts like chattel hunting and scavenging. Can you imagine he has resorted to devouring the remains of my discarded creations. The creatures that I forged as a novice in my works. A solid look of remorse and pity drew over the king's face. "I was ambitious, young and impatient," God confessed looking up at Tree. "Had you witnessed the look of defeat on Adam's face when he first discovered himself a tenant amongst the land of those ex-communicated and un-welcomed."

I remember the moment clearly," God admitted, "when Adam was confronted with the realization that he had been thrown out and discarded placed amongst the lowliest of beasts. I could feel his stock and sense of self-worth slowly diminishing. It did not take him long before he began to assume the port of his lowly station believing himself to be no different from the others. Adam began to view and see himself as being similar if not less valuable than those abandoned creatures roaming the lands before him." The tears that God held back as he spoke managed to escape rolling slowly down the side of his face. God eloquently stroked the canvas of his thoughts with an emotional paintbrush which help to illustrate his feelings.

"I wanted desperately to yell out to him, somehow remind him of his value and worth." "And what would you have said to him?" Tree gently probed, pardoning her intrusion. "Onto him I would have said. My child, do not assume yourself to be stale when you are indeed ripened or believe yourself a commoner when you are truly royalty." Tree was rather impressed by her king's affirmation. "Do not let this ungodly world severe you from your heritage. Do not allow yourself to be hoodwinked or fooled into accepting the nuances of a mundane and dismal life. You are greater and more powerful than you appear or imagine, I can attest to your greatness for you are my son, my greatest design."

God concluded his heartfelt admission; however, he could not look up at Tree. He felt somewhat helpless and vulnerable in his transparent state. "Yes," Tree reassured her king, "Adam is indeed your greatest creation without a doubt. He is unquestionably a creature to be reckoned with. Why not just call out to him..." asked Tree wielding sympathy in her regard. " I do not know!" replied the king somewhat defensive in his response "I did not call out to Adam because I still hold a personal grudge and resentment against him. I could already foresee beforehand the heated confrontation that would have ensued between us." "But why?" Tree pleaded, somehow already knowing the answer. God appeared symptomatic and deeply afflicted by his own pride and arrogance. Even though pride was one of the seven sins banned and outlawed by God, his inflated ego caused him to exercise immunity and exemption from his own legislation with no impunity. "It was my pride," God confessed openly "that would not let allow me to speak or call out to him at the time." Tree was humbled by the sincerity and honesty of her king's words. It was at this point that moisture and soft dew began to fill both their eyes.

"The command and mastery of love" God began to explain, "is a powerful instrument that when harnessed correctly it has the potential to charge and enhance as latent energy." Tree listened on with growing interest and intrigue at God's admission hoping to understand the reason and purpose for this telling. "Do you want to know the secret ingredient that I used to perfect Adam? God teased jovially "Yes," begged Tree most certainly eager and interested to learn the secrets and works of spiritual alchemy.

"Love." laughed out the king, but Tree was not amused but rather confused. "I do not understand," replied Tree. "Do not all creatures in Eden possess the ability to love, is that not the reason why we are able get along and cohabitate? "Yes, of course," answered the king smiling back noticing the growing interest on Tree's face regarding the topic and subject of spiritual metaphysics. "Alright Tree," God insisted, "I will share the secret recipe to creating life, but you must promise to never share this knowledge with any another creature or soul. "Why yes, of course, your majesty I would never betray your trust I am your loyal servant and confidant."

"Love is a finite element" God revealed, "it is the primary ingredient in which I use to conjure and create life. Love is the essential mineral of which I rinse and bathe all my creatures and creations. Love is embedded into the very fabric and essence of my architectural designs. Love as a stable component has the sustainable potential and capability to vitalize any creature or life force. Love serves as natural commodity of renewable energy which I use to charge and fuel all my creations. These creatures eventually learn to produce the essential minerals through small increments and fragments of gratitude. The qualifying production of the transparent minerals are collected and afterwards and stored for future harvest. They happily take stock in offering their gratitude, and appreciation by way of credit and merit. My creations graciously turn over the bulk of their love and admiration in the form and prayers worship. The continuous cycle can only sustain if my creations continue offer me their worship and praise. I have managed for centuries to stock and store massive quantities of the precious mineral. The invigorating potion has helped me to maintain my reign of power. Love being the anthesis of fear strengthens me to become mightier and more influential ruler."

Tree was shocked by God's confession and more confused by her master's admission. Though not fully oriented with the celestial roles and duties of her master. Tree did not pretend as if she fully understood or comprehended the complexity or vastness of her kings reasoning. The transformative process comprised of spiritual alchemy which allowed one to channel love into another spiritual being or energy life source. "Is this the reason and purpose of our existence?' Tree inquired reluctantly, "The creatures of the Eden, love me, because I provide sanctuary, and refuge. I give my creations a carefree life with very little hurdles or obstacles to overcome. I grant them access to nourishment and give abundantly by way of provisions. I created Eden to be a haven somewhat as an alternative to heaven. A place and paradise where all my creatures can safely call their home. And in return all that I ask is that they embrace me with affection and to shower me with their praises. It is the love and admiration that I receive from my loyal creations that fortifies and replenishes me." Tree was mesmerized and somewhat astonished to learn of her kings' insatiable obsession. She did not know how to respond and thought it best to remain silent yet attentive of the kings' words

"I have witnessed Adam growing stronger, and more powerful from the admiration and love that he receives from his family." God turned to Tree, looking directly into her face, "I always imagined that it would be myself and none other who would help guide Adam in discovering and harnessing the powerful of love. He somehow, managed to discover on his own the untapped potential of the raw mineral and how to transform it into a tangible material." God turned his head away in defeat, "It seems present circumstances have disqualified me from teaching him the profound lesson on responsibility, and accountability. Even you Tree, whether aware of the fact have received more love and enrichment from Adam, than I have as Adams's creator and founder."

God's vulnerability brought with it air of silent awkwardness over them. Tree wrestled with her nerves as she struggled to produce the appropriate answer or response. "But what should I say," she thought to herself, "what can I say?" Like Tree, the king was consumed and buried beneath the weight of deep thought and ponderance over the matter. "I can recall," God shared openly. "Seeing the radiant glow of accomplishment drawn across Adam face the first time he discovered fire. The memory remains to this day one of my proudest moment as his architect and creator. It confirmed my suspicion that I had designed a and crafted a remarkable being. Man was able to adapt and thrive successfully despite being placed in unaccommodating conditions. Adam was the only creature whose innate fear of the dark drove him to conjure up and create fire as a substitute and byproduct of light." The wayward direction of God's acknowledgement began to lift Tree's enthusiasm and spirits surrounding the issue of Adam. Though there were some valid truths to God's remarks pointing out Adam's open affection and preference for Tree over himself. Tree was not offset by the kings' remarks and continued to listen with growing interest. "I often wished that I had been active and present in Adam's life supportive of his crowning achievements and grand accomplishments. I would remain inglorious in my conviction and belief if I have not denied Adam his birthright as a demigod. Adam having been crafted from the sovereign powers of divinity was able to harness the unseen elements. The comprehension of nature and chemistry are forever embedded in Adam's biological blueprint. The sacred knowledge of chemistry, alchemy, and science were embedded within Adam curious mind with grand hope that knowledge and wisdom and the pursuit of understanding would help to ease the ascension and willingness to accept of his destined role as a demigod."

The king concluded his lengthy speech seeming somewhat uneasy and troubled by his present dilemma. The eerie awkwardness of silence began once again to fill the void between the two. Tree decided to offset the swelling tension by removing any discomfort and uneasiness felt between them. The king's admission though starchy and dry served as a compliment describing Adams fondness and admiration for her. Tree felt compelled to respond and offer her king some wisdom and council on the matter.

"Adam is indeed a most marvelous creature," Tree stated openly, "he has matured and developed well. His journey has brought him a long way from where he began. He has managed to secure and source the precious mineral in which you have come to describe as love. Adam has become domesticated and overly dedicated to the preservation of his partner and child. His son Cain resembles an exact image and replica of Adam at his youthful age. Adam and his family appear abundantly wealthy having been enriched with the rare mineral. They harvest and give love freely to each other in an endless cycle of admiration and appreciation. I see the impact and effect of the potent mineral much clearer now. Love is essentially the substance which fuels and powers Adams very lifeforce and existence. Adam is no longer the young infant that you proudly bestowed upon me..." Tree paused to glance at her king's face and found him listening attentively as though feeding pallidly from the discourse of her observation and views on the matter.

"Adam has become you." Tree boldly stated. "He unknowingly yearns to fulfill the godly role and honor the values in which you instilled within him. However, you attest his mate and even worse you profess that the creature is not of your making or design..." Tree, looked up again to gauge God's temperature in response to her remarks, and discovered that she had somehow bruised if not offended her king in her probing speech and insinuations. "Are you questioning my word?" God demanded, somewhat uneasy by Trees subtle and somewhat convert line of questioning. "Are you saying that I am somehow..." "No! your highness... of course not by no means..." Tree stammered nervously and quickly withdrew her suspicion retracting the very notion and idea. She did not wish to offend her king by challenging his words as anything other than irrefutable truth. "I mean no disrespect to you, my lord. I can assure you that is not my intention to provoke or chastise you. I only wish to state that which is already obvious to you that is Adam will never forsake his family. He appears very much happy if not content in his current station. His family feeds from what you describe as the sustainable energy of love which in turn helps their bond to grow stronger. Adams present fate has become enmeshed and deeply intwined in the honor and duty of provider-ship. I doubt very strongly that he is willing to depart and abandon his role and risk severing the dynamic bond he has formed and created with family; especially with the addition of Cain and mention of more."

"More!" God repeated loudly with devastation and disdain etched in his tone. Stroking his face gently caressing the hairs beneath his chin. His fingers grazing over the length of his silvery beard. God contemplated deeply considering for some time before responding to Tree's observation and assessment. "Yes, I see it clearly now," answered God. "Your assertions are correct. It appears that the devil is truly a worthy foe and adversary. He has somehow managed to transform my triumphant dream into a defeating nightmare. The devil has soiled my plans once again by way of theft and larceny. The wretched angel has changed if not disrupted the fabric of reality. My greatest creation Adam has somehow emancipated himself abandoning his ascension and plight. And now with the addition of Cain, his strength and power will increase. I fear that if left unchecked Adam will continue to multiply his power and grow..." "Wait," interrupted Tree, attempting to redirect the course of their engagement. "With all due respect your highness you cannot assume that Adam has been converted or somehow compromised. He is a simple trinket and pawn in an unholy war being waged between two adversaries. Adam is an unwilling participant in a long-standing feud between two powerful and opposing forces, good and evil."

God felt the affront of Tree's remarks but chose not to respond prematurely and instead listened to her defense with earnestness and sincerity, "Adam is not entirely at fault," Tree, continued, "In my eyes he has done nothing wrong and only seeks to fulfill his role as protector, and provider of his family." Tree hesitated a short moment, but quickly collected her composure to restate the premise of her argument. "Your highness, I do not believe your child, has left the realms of good nor do I believe he realizes that their even exists such realms. Your gift of love is embedded within him serving as the sail and ore that encompasses the path and direction of his journey." God could have easily silenced Tree at any moment with a simple gesture such as a snap of his finger, or a wave of a hands but did not. God decided that he would not interject or oppose Tree in the middle of her swelling and passionate plea. He was assured that she would eventually blunder over her emotions and reveal her true thoughts and feelings.

"The child Cain is a product of Adam, who is indeed a product of you. By that logic it makes sense to say that Cain is your kin," Her words stunned the king, for God had never given much thought or consideration to the dichotomy their complicated relationship. Adam is your son; therefore, his son should belong to you as well." Tree was proud of herself, she felt as though she had made a breakthrough with connecting her point to her king "I conclude with final point," she argued "If Adam, is fully bred with the lineage of royal goodness, then it can be presumed that his son and offsprings will inherently possess half if not a quarter of those good traits and qualities within them. The idea and notion of inherited goodness should serve as a source of refuge and comfort. It should inspire reassurance and hope for Adam's lineage and future off springs. I firmly believe that goodness and love will reign supreme and that the forces of evil will eventually dwindle and overtime to become an inequitable and obsolete force.

God understood very well Tree's intent in attempting to remove doubt and reservations held around Adam's loyalty. However, the king was not fully convinced and refused to dismiss his preconceived suspicions. "I have heard your appeal," God responded, "and though you may offer some viable points in Adams defense, I assure you that your optimistic outlook is an overly simplistic conclusion. I will excuse your misguided understanding of the present situation and pardon your lack of comprehension surrounding celestial forces." Tree was shocked somewhat taken aback by the subtle slight of her master insults. "Since the dawn of time, I have designed and curated an unfathomable number of creatures many of which were created before your time. Through my trials and experience I have come to improve and discern the extent of my own power and craft."

"My dear friend..." God paused abruptly looking directly at Tree with stern seriousness drawn on his face, "It is impossible for two or more forces to embody one entity coexisting simultaneously without disfunction and trepidation infecting the heart and spirit of its host. No matter if the creature is half bred, or quarter fledged the undeniable fact remains that evil still exists enmeshed deep within the fabric of the creature's design. Even if a fraction of inherent goodness is adopted by his offsprings the substantial imbalance of evil will eventually prevail as the dominant force.

"Evil is an extremely volatile force," explained the king "much more infectious than the powers of good and love. Evil is a silent cancer that grows deep within the bowels of its host like a parasite. Sin has helped to corrupt the very fabric of my creation filling him with inadequacy for his lowly transgressions. Evil can remain dormant for centuries within its host and wait patiently for the perfect moment or opportunity to reveal and unfurl itself." Tree seemed uneasy by her king's message and considered on the possible fate and outcome of Adam. "No," Tree declared openly refusing and unwilling to accept God's logic as infinite truth, "I cannot imagine Adam directing his son into the abyss of evil and darkness. In my observation Adam has been nothing but kind and nurturing keeping a watchful eye over his mate and child. He will ensure that Cain does not fall into grips with evil."

Tree appeared disturbed and utterly rattled by the density of her king's objections. "I understand your concerns and sympathize with your cause." God announced, "The inevitable truth remains that life in the barren wasteland will only help to exacerbate and fuel the dormant evil spirit within. The negative force will eventually overshadow the inherent kindness and goodness founded during the creature's birth. His warm heart will become hardened and cold as he learns to navigate through this world filled with pain and strife. Adam was raised and brought up in the hospitable and comfortable world of Eden. Cain however will be reared in the unsavory conditions of bedrocks and flatlands. It was never my intention or plan for any of my creations to inhabit let alone endure life in this bedrock of wilderness."

"So let him return home." Tree urged. "Allow Adam to return to come back to Eden with his mate and child. Exonerate him and pardon of his sins, and transgressions by allowing his family to enter..." "No!!!" declared the king in a defiant tone, "I will do no such thing." God refused with a haughty tone and temperament. I will not stand idle and allow my perfect garden and paradise to be overrun by vile and evil forces. Adam's future offsprings will eventually taint if not compromise the integrity of my perfect oasis."

Tree feared she had upset her king and aroused his violent temper; God's voice retained a stern and firm tone. He spoke with deliberate precision ad clarity. "My creations are products of purity, and goodness, wholesomeness, and worthiness," Tree wrestled with her nerves attempting desperately to sooth her king's temper. "Please your highness," Tree pleaded, offering the king an apology for her poorly chosen words and remarks. However, Tree's apology and poor attempt to shift the direction of their conversation went unnoticed by the contemptuous and enraged king. Tree considered the thought of challenging and speaking out against the blaring sound of God's voice. She appeared unnerved by the overwhelming reaction and sound of the king which seem to detain and paralyze Tree. She found herself placed in a state of duress which suppressed her urge to freely speak her mind.

The passion of God was a heartfelt and deafening sound to experience and behold. He dismissed Tree's assertions viewing them as trifle sentiments of an advantageous and favorable caretaker and nothing more. "I must get Adam back." God affirmed openly, "I must prevent him from falling into the grips of evil for I fear that my nemesis has hatched a plan." "A plan?" echoed Tree, recovering her voice and speaking out. "Yes." God answered. "It is my fear that evil forces will use Adam to create an army of damnable creatures to reign over the world which I have carefully crafted and curated. Adams descendants will be formed morally bankrupt and filled with vileness and corruption. They will work devotedly to the destruction and degradation of my work. His children and descendants if left unchecked will eventually fall into service and alignment with evil. Their vile sentiments and attraction to organized corruption and destruction only help to demonstrate their unwavering allegiance to the dark side."

Tree was taken aback by the king's sense of militancy. God resembled a commander of high ranks exploring complex strategies in preparation for combat and warfare. "Today they are three," God warned. "But in time you will find that Adam will produce many more offsprings. The small creatures will eventually grow into a small army and eventually form a large brigade. I dread to consider the rate at which his children and decedents will grow." God imagined for a moment the unfathomable numbers of souls that would flood the heavenly gate. "I foresee a tidal wave of evil souls clashing like waves in effort to breach the heavenly gates of my fortress. What will I do then Tree?" God asked absurdly. "When these unjust souls bent on overthrowing my kingdom begin to gather and outnumber the calvary of my winged angels. What shall I do then, Tree? Who will I have to stand at my side to help fight back against the rebellion?"

A fearsome shudder overtook Tree. She appeared rattled by the context of her king's inquisitions. The sudden hard shake prompted a few leaves and fruits to drop and fall off from her branches. Tree had never considered the full weight and magnitude of Adam's fate and existence on such massive scale. "I apologize your highness for I had no idea," Tree pleaded her ignorance to her king with genuine earnestness and passion. "Please my lord, I do not wish to see evil reign over this world or any other world. My lord, if there is any way that I can be of assistance, possibly serving as an anchor of support, please tell me. I am but your humble servant." God was pleased to hear Tree's words. Her unyielding obedience and loyalty to the greater cause was deemed grand and good. God was slowly beginning to regain the trust and confidence he had once placed over Tree, assuming that she was indeed offering her allegiance willfully. This time God was determined more than ever not to severe the ties of their bond.

God seized the moment of solidarity as the perfect opportunity and time to unfurl his ingenious plot to win Adam back. "When Adam comes to visit you again, you will ask him to give you a lock of his mate's hair..." but before God could finish his sentence, Tree quickly, countered with an inquiry. "But how do you suppose I will get him to give me the hair?" Tree asked, seeming rather puzzled by the request. "I mean, what would I possibly need with a lock of..." Tree became silent after glancing up to find the intolerable look of annoyance drawn on her master's face. Utilizing keen intellect and good observational skills, Tree decided to stop speaking to allow for her king to continue. "You test my patience," warned her master "you would be wise to avoid such buffoonery." Tree recognized with clarity as to the nuance of her kings' impassive threats. "I do not wish to test your temper your highness, but how should I explain is the reason for my desire or need to possess the lock of hair? "Tree proposed humbly.

God paused briefly to consider Tree's qualm. It was apparent by his silence that the plot had been prematurely conceived. The plan was not fully flushed out, God had not considered the intricate details necessary to complete and fulfill his masterful scheme. A moment of hesitation passed before the king answered. "You can present your request as a tokened reward. The subtle request should not trigger suspicion or arouse any alarm but instead be perceived as an honorary gesture. An act of appreciation for several decades of fostering and waiting over him. The request for a locket of hair should appear meaningless and rather credulous to Adam serving as nothing more than a strange and rather innocent request."

Tree, wanted to pose another question to God, however the king responded to her inquiry before she could speak out. "If Adam asks you as to why you desire the lock of hair, tell him not to worry, and that he should trust you and not question or second guess your request..." Tree was put off and somewhat unsettled by the shrewd callousness of her king's recommendation. Tree felt an air of distress with addressing Adam in such a rash and evasive manner. A perplexing combination of emotions flooded throughout her body. Tree felt emotionally torn; she knew it was wrong to betray the relationship and trust of her dearest and closest friend Adam. A heavy feeling of resentment overcame Tree as she was being forced to face the fact that she reserved no ownership or free will to escape or refuse the conspiring proposition. Tree felt resentful of her stationary disposition which did not allow her the animation or mobility to run away and flee. Tree found it especially challenging if not difficult to go against or disobey her masters wishes.

As Tree listened on to the intricate details of the king's elaborate plot, she could not help but feel a heavy of as sense of guilt, and shame weighing over her shoulders. Tree begrudgingly listened with the impeding sense and urge to speak out against his plan. No longer able to contain her impulse Tree spoke out of turn. "With all due respect, and honesty" Tree interjected, "I am truly uncomfortable with this plan which possess more like a rouse and somewhat of a sham." Tree was nervously aware understanding how the implications of her words could easily be misinterpreted and taken as contempt by the king. Tree was however brave and unflinching standing up firm in her beliefs ready to embrace the unforeseen outcome. Her trembling voice began to slowly draw momentum growing more audacious and bolder.

"I would prefer to remain as I am, neutral, and free from any bad tidings against Adam. I am sorry my lord, but I refuse to be a subject in this ploy." Tree quickly recalled her disposition of servitude and aligned accordingly by disarming her rebellious tone. She exchanged her words, applying a much subtle approach. "My king" Tree humbled, "you know I cannot force Adam, to obey such an order," God, was stricken, by Tree's refusal, "for unlike myself Adam wields the gift of free will, he has the freedom and autonomy un-afforded by any other creature. Adam can simply refuse my request..." But before Tree could finish her thought, "Silence!!!" God exploded in a loud and startling uproar, "How dare you offer you defiance and question your allegiance to me!" God's tone was rough and stern harshly untamed but effectively intimidating and uneasy to endure.

The suppressed emotions which lived dormant within Tree began to slowly resurface. The fearsome wrath of God began to suddenly stir within her. "No!" God answered irrefutably. "Adam is not free, and you are not free, none of my creations are free. You all belong to me." The king declared "Look around everything you that you see belongs to me." Tree was shaken by the brashness of her master's words. She desperately wanted to dissolve her master's anger with a heartfelt apology but this time it was too late. A genuine apology would be of little use in resolving her master's contentions.

Tree accidentally caused her king anguish upsetting him beyond the point of forgiveness. God was no longer receptive to Tree's pleas ignoring her offers of remorse. Tree's apologies and pleas no longer helped to suffice or convince the angry king. The only thing that would diminish God's anguish was if Tree consented and agreed to comply and assist with the unfurling of his intricate plot. God chastised Tree in a demanding and assertive tone "You side against me?" God questioned rhetorically. "Even after I have opened up and disclosed to you the severity of the situation. Do you wish for evil to conquer over good? Do you want to see the raid of countless sullied souls barging against the gates of heaven? Can you fathom the thought of seeing your king and master overthrown and removed from my high rank of my present station?"

Tree did not wish to see any of God's rhetoric's come to fruition. The very idea filled her with shuttering fright. She trembled nervously at the daunting images which filled her mind. "Nooo!" Tree cried out hysterically, "I do not wish to see evil win or reign supreme. I only wish to serve your highness..." God's could easily observe the distressing look of fear on Tree's face, and slowly began to adjust his tone. His intention was not to frighten or startle Tree, but rather to instill a sense of urgency and necessity regarding the fate of man.

In a soft and calming voice God reminded Tree of her historic request to support Adam. "You pled to be placed here in the outskirts so that you may continue to support and watch over Adam, and did I not honor your request?" However, before Tree could answer or respond God, continued., "You implored for me to share the golden apple to aide Adam back to health, which he then used to feed and restore his mate as well. I was aware of Adam's plot, but out of respect and consideration to you I chaperoned the idea. I granted your wish and produced onto you the golden apple that saved Adams life. So, then tell me good friend, why is your cause any nobler than mine? Why do you refuse to support me in my effort to save Adam's life?"

Tree listened to Gods message with childlike remorse absorbed internally against a host of racing thoughts. She contemplated the moral implications and the significance in assisting in completing Gods plan. Tree was quickly reminded of her subservient station, as her decision to assist would be volunteered by the king's next few words. "I will have Adam back!" Bluntly exclaimed the king, "With or without your assistance." A shattering look of disappointment and defeat appeared over Tree's face as she sought desperately to reproach her king but failed miserably. "You may be his guardian," The king concluded abruptly "Do not forget that your allegiance to me supersedes your alliance with anyone or any other being."

The king's threat of permanent removal was enough to force Tree into a place of submission. She chose to end the storm of feuding words between herself and the king. Tree expelled a deep sigh of remorse from deep within the pits of her soul. "Please forgive me." Tree pled desperately. "I will accept your will and do as you desire." However, it was much too late for Tree. It seemed that God was now filled with staggering indifference and behaved callously toward his regarded friend. He no longer held Tree in high regard, but now looked on at his friend as fickle and unreliable. "I suggest you do what is best for your own sake," God warned in a cold dismissing tone. "Your very existence may very well depend on your decision." At hearing his warning Tree felt distraught recognizing very well the full extent and implication of the king's passive threat. Tree had never known her king to not fulfill his promises especially those that entailed fatal outcomes.

"So now I have provided you with a plausible motive," God concluded to his crony. "You may now request for the locket of hair as though the outcome was pertinent and vital to your very existence." Without another word uttered, his majesty suddenly disappeared in the same manner and fashion that he appeared. Tree found herself once again alone in the company of her private thoughts pondering considerably over the pressing ordeal of her present circumstances. She began to slowly unravel breaking down into wanton tears. "Woe, is me" Tree cried out, "I fear that dark times draw near with peril and misfortune to follow. I wish not to be a syndicate of oppression or be in any way complicit in this foul and nefarious scheme." Tree cried out pleading openly into the silent night air but receiving no response. The debilitating feelings of helpless and hopelessness began to form like soft resin of dew over her eyes. Beads of moist tears filled her eyes before cascading down her brittle face. Tree could not stop or control the rush of tears from pouring down her face. She felt hopeless to expose or wipe away her brooding look sadness drawn over her dampened face. Her limitation to do so served to further the panging insult and humiliation. Tree was left with no other course of action other than to rely on the cool breeze and night air to dry her tears. On this night Tree bathed herself in a hailstorm of fluttering tears. Tree cried and wept piteously the entire night until pacified by the overwhelming sensation and urge to pursue rest and secure sleep.

The Conspirator

With the plot steady unfurling in the background all seemed to be going as planned. However, Tree was still uneasy. Lost and without direction, Tree found her moral compass shattered and somewhat compromised. She wrestled against her conscious and struggled to sleep and rest on many nights. The afternoons and evenings afforded her no peace of mind enduring the same restless thoughts. "I am disgraced by my dishonesty," Tree admitted to herself feeling truly shameful, and uneasy of her act. "I exist solely as a puppet of mischief strung forth by the mighty puppeteer and king." Tree had unwittingly assumed the diplomatic role and position as ambassador becoming the bridge connecting father and son. Tree was still uncomfortable with idea of being utilized as a pawn in the plot to defiling and unbraiding her dear friend Adam. "I am but a simple slave forced to obey a master so cruel and unforgiving." Tree would go on like this for several days without cessation or adequate rest. The absence of sleep became apparent and could be observed by way of her sluggish and lethargic demeanor. Trees bright leaves which once flourished with vigor and chlorophyl were no longer green. Instead, they carried rustic a copper and rustic tone. Tree accepted that what she was doing was wrong and scolded her-self daily for making the fallacious request.

Tree wept pitifully this for several days in deliberation and council of her thoughts. "It was not my will nor was it my intention to deceive and betray my dearest friend, the one to whom I hold the closest bond." The gnawing sense of deception, and dishonesty seem to eat away at her taking an emotional toll over Tree as she wept daily. Tree went on like this for several days shouldering the weight of her sorrows. She could be observed weeping incessantly, her tears stretching through the day and settling only after nightfall. Tree could not escape her thoughts, nor could she keep from reliving her encounter with Adam ruminating over the very act of her betrayal. Tree felt tormented and pled secretly for death to make a swift end of her life. Tree secretly reserved the morbid hope that she would perish before Adam's return simply to avoid appearing deceptive and impartial in her judgment. She desired to escape the burden of guilt, free from the implication of having assisted and betrayed either father, or son.

God was masterfully executing his plan at the expense of Tree's health and well-being. Tree could feel her energy fading, her health depleting and becoming worse with furthering of days. The insidious and poisonous thoughts Tree fostered were beginning to cause detrimental if not devastating effects on her mind and body. The visible result could be observed through the deterioration of her overall health and condition. "I detest most of all, this slow and agonizing demise." Tree cursed out loud, feeling disoriented and dazed. "Why not end my suffering and be done with me already!" She hoped to provoke a response from her tormentor but instead found her woeful grievance's unanswered her woeful outcries fallen on deaf ears.

One brisk evening just before nightfall as Adam was resting in his home. A thought of Tree surfaced in his mind as he was reminded of his promise. He had postponed and missed several appointments to see her. Adam felt burdened with overwhelming guilt in realizing that he had not seen or visited Tree for some time. Adam set out to visit Tree, not before securing the lock of hair that she had so humbly requested. The moon seemed to glow bright on this night, while the glittering stars seem to shimmer and sparkle lighting up night. The cluster of twinkles and ambient lighting from the moon presence offered a guiding light for Adam to trail. Adam trooped peacefully through the night like a soldier making his way unaffected and undeterred by the weariness of the night.

The distant pathway leading to Tree was a familiar route in which Adam instinctively memorized having chartered and traveled the beaten path many times. As he got closer Adam placed his sight on a strange and unfamiliar object off in the distance. He appeared somewhat confused by the questionable figure standing before him. Adam was uncertain as to whether the strange shadowy image was an illusion of his senses.

Adam spotted what he presumed to be Tree beneath the budding light of the moon. He could scarcely make out the familiar face he had grown accustomed to seeing. Tree appeared decrepit and hunched over, with a questionable crease in her posture. Adam began his slow pace walking towards Tree drawing suspicion with every step. He seemed troubled and confused by the unexplainable outcome of his friend's condition. The glowing moon illuminating high above the gentle sky failed to provide the necessary light to improve his sight and senses to make a clear distinction. Adam appeared riddled if not perplexed by Trees ailing condition and outward appearance. An uncontrollable sense of fear suddenly gripped Adam causing him to stop in his tracks. He felt uneasy and somewhat frightened standing before the strange creature and ended his dissent. Adam standing only a few meters from the unfamiliar object decided to call out to it. "Tree is that you?" Adam shouted into the air. The familiar voice rang like an alarm awakening Tree from her decrepit slumber.

Tree attempted to unfasten her eyes but discovered that she was far too tired and exhausted to open them. Her replenished and youthful state was temporary if not brief. Engulfed in grief and self-loathing Tree adopted depravation as her formal mindset. Tree refused to eat or sleep the act of self-torment was evidenced by the dryness of her chaffed and worn-down skin. The layered texture of her bark coating appeared flimsy and drooped down giving the appeared of a hunched body. The branches of her crown clung desperately to the few remaining strands of ruffling leaves left on her head. Tree heard Adam's voice, calling out to her and struggled with much effort to awaken from her slumbering state. She finally managed to pry open her eyes only to rejoice at discovering that it was indeed Adam standing before her. At first observation she believed Adam to be a hallucination and dream of some sorts cast from depths of her imagination as an active delusion. Trees frail body trembled involuntarily while staring directly into Adam's worried face. She wanted to speak out and say something to him but found it impossible to muster the strength. Her voice was hoarse, and dry her words resembled indistinguishable utterances whenever she attempted to speak. Adam could scarcely make sense of her words and encouraged Tree to rest to restore her energy. However, Tree did not stop and continued her attempt to communicate and speak out. Overcome with sadness Adam dropped to his knees drawing his face closer to hear Tree, but still struggling to not make out what she was saying.

"Adam, is that you?" Tree whispered softly in a stale dry voice "you... have... returned...". "Yes." Adam answered rejoicing, "I have not forsaken you. I have returned, just as I promised, and look," Adam began rummaging through his satchel and clothes in search of the special object. "I have come back bearing a gift for you." He managed retrieve the object from deep within the confines of his wooly garments. Adam revealed the locket of hair, but Tree could hardly set her sights to gaze upon it. "Tell me Tree," Adam began to plead, "what is wrong, what form illness has befallen you?" "No," Tree answered, 'I am dying," Tree announced." Her cold words brought a shudder through his entire body, "I do not think I will be around for much longer." The sound of growing decay festered in her voice. "Dddying." Adam stuttered over his words overcome with an intensity and emotion. "But I do not understand." Adam questioned pleading his ignorance in the matter. The thought of losing his matriarch and best friend was a heart wrenching for Adam to endure. The swelling thought grief and loss brought tears to his face. "Are you sick?" Adam cried out. "Is there anything that I can do?" He began to beg and plead standing over Tree's stretched out body. Adam began to panic. "Please do not leave me!" He cried out repeatedly while sobbing uncontrollably. His moistened face drenched with a combination of tears and mucus that ran down his sobbing face.

It overwhelmed Adam to feel so helpless unable to intervene or provide any assistance or support. A mixture of emotions flooded Adams body overwhelming his senses and nerves. He instantly blamed himself for Tree's condition. "If only I had not delayed my visit." Adam berated and taunted himself. "If only I had come to visit her earlier, and not tarried my stay." Tree fought to hold back her tears but could not suppress the flow of water that began to spill down her face. Watching Adam badgering and blaming himself made Tree feel even more guilty and shameful for her treacherous behavior. In the twilight of her deathbed Tree wished more than anything for enough energy to speak out and clear her conscious. If possible, she would confess the entire arrangement between the king, and herself. Tree would have done anything at the time to offer relief to Adam and unburden him from the burden of guilt he now carried over him. Despite all her good intentions and willing spirit Tree was much too tired and exhausted to speak up. She could only stare on with silent admiration entranced by the familiar face staring back at her.

Tree struggled with maintaining consciousness and fought desperately to stay awake. She feared that the worst would occur if she chose to close her eyes to rest. Adam put his arms around her body noticing how fragile and frail her body now seemed. He thought back to happier times when his arms could never reach or wrap around Trees strong bulky frame. Adam fastened the dead weight of her body in his arms and attempted against natural forces to try and erect her back up again. The task alone became a daunting struggle as the more Adam heaved to lift Tree upward, the heavier her trunk seemed weigh down over him.

He pushed and pulled tugged, and tilted until finally a loud cracking sound, came from her body, "Ouch! " Tree cried out, "please! stop!" The frightening sound of Trees body suddenly snapping, and breaking apart caused Adam to stop immediately and end his attempts to lift and prop Tree back up. Adam gently laid Tree back down to the floor returning her back to the awkward position and crippling state he discovered her. Adam seeming very much displeased by the situation became paralyzed with tension and frustration. Adam grew quiet and stoic at best exhausting much of the anger and frustration in his mind. In silent and deep thought Adam scoured the corners and crevices of his mind searching desperately for to a way to help Tree regain her life force and avoid a senseless end. He grazed over her branches, and limbs recalling a time when they felt firm and strong but now, they were brittle and old. The radiant flow of green leafy hair that distinguished Tree was no longer her featured attribute. Most of her leaves had shed and were scattered about on the ground around her. Only patches of dry clumpy leaves clung to what remained of her Trees head.

Adam did not fully comprehend what was happening to his friend but garnered his suspicions. "I cannot imagine the lengths to which solitude and loneliness exacerbated your decay. It has spoiled and rotted you from the core within. I am sorry that I could not give to you a companion to share your days..." Adam spoke as if spiritually ordained in the ministry and service of his dear friend. "I am sorry," he continued, "for my neglect, and for not visiting you more often. I had no idea the extent and severity to which seclusion, and isolation plagued you terribly. And had I not been so thoughtless, and shortsighted, I would surely have taken notice of your ailing's." Tree lay silently resting in Adams arms in absence of words looking on wearily as though struggling to stay with him. She could no longer manage to stay awake and rolled her eyes back into the dark curtains of her eyelids signifying her fateful resignation and end. Tree stayed lucid long enough to hear most of Adams kind and generous words. However, she was unable to enjoy the entire ceremony and would not make it to the end of his beautiful eulogy.

Shortly after Trees passing something amazing began to happen. The very sky began to sever and open revealing a beam of bright light that shone down gleaming over Adam and his befallen friend. "I see that you truly love and care for Tree," sounded a proud and ominous voice. It was God, who was now speaking to Adam. God had been quietly watching Adam, and Tree observing the entire interaction from high above. He was looking down at them listening and waiting for the perfect moment to come forth and speak out. "Will you miss her?" God asked Adam, rhetorically as if unaware as of his response. "Yes!" Adam cried out in bellowing loud voice. The numbing pain of losing Tree seemed to impact Adam desensitizing him from the fact that he was being engaged and comforted by his creator and father. "Do not worry my son," God reassured Adam, "you will not see Tree perish for I will save her from this tragic fate." Adam was surprised by his father's generous offer and marveled at the kindness and benevolence of the king. Adam wiped his face clean with his palms removing any evidence or reminisce of his tears. "I will bring Tree's body back with me into Eden where she belongs so that she may recover and regain, her vitality."

The news of Tree's removal brought with it great despair as Adam no longer seemed excited. "But why?" Adam inquired, "How will I be able to see Tree? Have you forgotten," Adam reminded his father. "That you have banished and barred me from ever returning home." God was a little irritated and taken back by the sharpness of Adams wit and the audaciousness of his tone. "No, I have not forgotten." God responded calmly "however in consideration of present circumstances, I am willing to temporarily relinquish your sentence and restore your access to Eden. You will be free to venture in and out of the grand walls as frequently as you please."

Adam was moved by the kings offer to revoke the ban that would allow him safe passage and access into the garden. "Wait," Adam hesitated, "you are willing to let me travel back and forth freely through Eden as I please?" "Yes," answered the king, "I am allowing it so that you may continue to see and visit our dear friend. It is my hopes that the sight of you will help to aide Tree on her path to recovery." Adam gave a cheerful smile as he had been somewhat touched by the sentimental gesture of his father. He began to reconsider his position and began to welcome the idea of ending their long-standing feud. Adam was growing more receptive to the idea of reunification and the thought of visiting home and seeing the paradise once again. He found himself consumed in the moment flooded by a host of emotions. He had no idea that his yearning desire to help his dear friend would also serve as a pathway to reconciliation with his father. Adam was very much entranced by God's kindness and generosity that he was unable to clearly see the web of lies that the king was masterfully weaving.

"Thank you, father." Adam joyfully praised the king filling God with the rare and intoxicating mineral of love. "Tree, often declared you to be a kind and noble king. I am glad to learn that she was truthful in her telling's." Adam began to reconsider his initial stance in relation to his father. "Maybe I was wrong about him." Adam considered to himself before suddenly recalling his oath and promise to Tree. "Wait please!" Adam urged, requesting a moment from the king. He dug into the trenches of his shabby attire and shuffled about strangely until finally he secured the object. Adam pulled out his hands and extended his arms outward to the sky displaying the lock of hair enclosed between his fingers. Adam provided the reasonable explanation for the lock of hair and described the symptoms of loneliness and isolation which he deduced and diagnosed to be the cause of Tree's current state and condition. Adam offered God the locket of hair that he had promised to secure for Tree placing it directly from the temple and crown of his fallen friend. "Do not worry, Tree," Adam reassured leaning in close as to ensure that she clearly heard him, "I have advocated for your request my dear friend, and hopefully you will receive your companion." Adam in turning his attention back to the king began to once again address his father.

"Father, may I offer a solemn confession." Adam offered to the king. "Father." God repeated the unfamiliar phrase himself revering the title. Having been unaccustomed to being addressed by his nobility God was moved and somewhat filled him joy and love. "Yes, my son," God happily acknowledged. "Go on." Adam was moved by the reception of being addressed as son by his estranged father. "I find that I am unable to find the time to give Tree the proper care and attention that she desperately needs. I would like to ask that you create companion for Tree, a creature of my likeness and design. A friend with whom Tree could share her time and find companionship in the place of my absence. Please bestow onto Tree a loyal confidant and friend one that is as true and faithful to her as she has been to me." Adam was finally finished his long-winded plea and though his request was lengthy and extensive it was also very much sincere and heartfelt. Acting as instructed; Adam tied the lock of hair to one of Tree's nimble limbs. The warmth from Adams hand and touch managed to stirr Tree from her slumbering state. She slowly peeled her eyes apart only to meet the lock of hair dangling aimlessly inches away from her face.

Seeing the lock of hair Tree was immediately stricken with grief and turmoil, shame and remorse. She looked over at Adam with the expression of agony and heartbreak drawn over her face. The thought of remorse was hard for Tree to bear as watery tears began to spill and pour out endlessly from her corners of her eyes. Resentment of her implicit involvement manifested into feelings of resentment and bitterness towards God. Tree was disappointed with herself for having supported and corroborated in the king's fiendish plot. Endless tears streamed down Tree's face as she sought desperately to speak out and warn Adam against God's plan but could not the muster the strength. Her tears communicated loudly the regret and remorse that she now carried with her.

God on the other hand was very much satisfied with the present outcome and conclusion. He looked to be the victor and beneficiary of the entire ordeal, managing to both secure the lock of hair, while rekindling the strained relationship between himself and Adam. The king was very much pleased with the prospective outcome and trajectory of his plan and scheme. "I will do as you ask my son," God responded, "Tree shall have a companion, a creature to help nurse her back to health." With the lock of hair in his grasp nothing could stop God from continuing the next phase of his masterful scheme, and inglorious plan.

With no further words to exchange God started his work. The ground began to shake and tremble beneath his feet. The rumbling floor began break apart and split open exposing the extension of Tree's lower body and roots. Her thick coiled roots sprang out from beneath ground forcing a gust of dirt and debris to fly into the air. Tree began her ascension scaling upward carried forth by luminous light. The rapturing force elevated Tree into the air. She was preparing to be transported and returned home to Eden where she belonged. Hovering in the air Tree could see the barred gates of the grand wall opening before her. The bittersweet moment cast an air of despair and sadness over Adam watching Tree being hoisted back into paradise.

The barred gates pried open its doors to welcome and receive Tree back into Eden. Adam's interest and curiosity was peeked gazing in through the doorway. He felt somewhat like a spectator looking in from the outside. Despite his eager attempt Adam could only catch a brief glimpse of the fertile vast land. Adam marveled over the abundance of beauty and variation of colorful plants and flowers residing in the garden. He had almost forgotten how wonderfully mesmerizing Eden appeared. Adam was entranced by the various shades of greenery that existed in the garden. He felt a sense of nostalgia viewing the decorative flowers and shrubs that covered the landscape of Eden. The theme and motif of greenery seemed to thrive abundantly with grass stretching as far and wide as the eye can see. Adam had nearly forgotten the vast beauty of his homeland and observed the botanical environment with a refreshing sense of appreciation for the soft fertile grounds.

The task was complete Tree's body was safely secured inside of Eden. The large gates slammed shut once again barring it gates. The image of the garden brought back special feelings and childhood memories. Adam began to ruminate over joyful thoughts and fanciful moments of when he resided in Eden. It was not long before the memories began to fade, and Adam found himself standing alone and idol in the company of his own shadow.

It was nearing dawn, and sunlight was rapidly approaching. Now that Tree was gone, there was nothing but mortar and stone surrounding him. Even the small pasture of grass of which Tree stood upon was slowly decaying as the patched soil dirt began to dry and harden. Adam exhaled a heavy sigh of helplessness breathing out from nostrils. The task was complete there was nothing more left to done. He dropped his shoulders and turned around to begin his and journey back home. On his walk home Adam replayed over in his mind the events which had taken place. He found himself ambivalent and mixed with a variation of different emotions and feelings. Internally he wrestled with feelings of shame, guilt, anger, and resentment. These very emotions which plagued Tree began to fester and consume Adam's thoughts. He did not want to view the loss of Tree as a bleak and unfortunate situation but rather he chose instead to look optimistically over the outcome of their present circumstance. This thought helped to restore the sensation of joy and satisfaction that he regarded in his actions. Adams believed wholeheartedly that his advocacy served purposeful in helping to assist with saving the life of his dearest friend.

Adam's good intention and valor began to quickly dwindle as he shifted the gears of his wayward thoughts toward feelings of insecurity and self-centeredness. He began to consider his reception and how he would be met by the creatures and inhabitants of Eden. Much time had passed since Adam last stepped foot into the garden. He began to feel uncomfortable and somewhat uneasy with the notion and idea of returning to Eden. "But what will the creatures think?" He pondered anxiously over the subject of his homecoming. "How will they respond to my sudden appearance," Adam wondered, "especially after such a long and extended absence. Will they even remember who I am?" Adam questioned to himself with growing anxiety as to how he would be perceived upon his return home.

These trivial questions and pestering rhetoric's corralled the vacant space in Adam's head. The idea occupied his thoughts keeping him enthralled if not occupied on his long journey home. He ventured forth in private council and conference of his thoughts. Adam was seemingly grief stricken by the removal of his dear friend and matriarch. "Where will I turn when in need of guidance and wisdom." Adam pleaded openly with his thoughts. "Whom shall I now confide my most inner turmoil in exchange for kind and generous words of affirmation and wisdom" This was truly a monumental loss for Adam. He was unable to nominate a qualifying candidate suited to serve as Trees successor. Growing tired and exhausted of feeling bombarded and defeated Adam chose to reserve his criticism for a later time. He dismissed his racing thoughts actively choosing to travel home in silent honor and memory of his dear friend and confidante.

The Dichotomy

Seasons came and passed before Adam returned to visit and meet with Tree. He was kept busy managing the intricate affairs of his domestic and personal life. The dutiful roles of being both provider, and protector were positions in which Adam fulfilled with great honor and reverence. Every morning Adam traveled out of his cave in the search of wild game. Most evenings, he returned home successful bearing some form of sustenance for his family to savor and feast over.

However, today's hunt was proving to be unusually difficult for Adam with game being scarce. Despite his countless efforts and attempts Adam was unable to snag the simplest of prey. By midday he was ready to give up the hunt and collect his failed attempts and return home empty handed and defeated. Adam struggled internally somewhat haunted by the dreadful thought of returning home with nothing to offer but the weight of his pride and shame. These detouring thoughts and more caroled Adams mind denying him the satisfaction of accepting the compromising retreat. Adam became very much accustomed to supporting his family and intended to retain the title and merit of his position. The provider ship role demanded that Adam serve as a patron offering sponsorship and care over the wellbeing of his family. The highly esteemed position became a source of joy for Adam bringing purpose and fulfillment into his life and very existence.

Adam began to withdraw any hope of capturing a meal on this day and began to consider surprising his family with an alternative menu option namely fruit delectables. He recalled how much Cain had enjoyed the tasty fruits and resolved that a variation in diet was needed from their typical routine dinner. Adam soon found himself walking along the dusty trail engaged in council and dialogue of inner thoughts. His proactive sense of wanderlust was purposeful in helping him navigate and locate the pathway leading to Tree.

Adam eventually arrived at Tree's post and was very much excited to see his old friend. He was ready if not excited to unload a host of quarreling thoughts and rhetoric's. However he reconsidered the thought upon observing Tree's current state and demeanor, Adam could easily dispel and determine that Tree was not her usual cheerful self. Adam took notice to how withered and pale her thin bark shone. Drawing closer Adam placed his hands on her body and began caressing her face with his palms. Tree appeared fatigued and dehydrated beneath the scorching blaze of the merciless sun. Her design was no longer solid or sturdy, but instead frail and brittle. Where once stood a full stock of bouncy green hair was now nothing more than clumps of bushy patches and decayed rustic leaves. It became apparent at the time that Tree was troubled however the source of her ailments was unbeknown to Adam.

"Tree, are you alright?" Adam asked, "you do not seem to be your usual self." Tree did not answer, "Are you not well?" He quickly added hoping to prompt a response, hopefully an explanation as to her present condition. "Oh why, hello, Adam." Tree greeted Adam somberly sounding unenthused by his arrival. Adam was unaware that Tree was exhausted, and deprived. Her lack of sleep and rest was observed in her tired demeanor speaking softly. "I see you travel alone today, where is your loving appendage of a son, Cain...?" Trees playful inquiry helped to ease the tension of her racing mind. Her thoughts shifted back and forth offset by the weight of harbored emotions which she festered over daily. Tree was bombarded daily with haunting thoughts of betrayal. She often contemplated as to whether she would be able to commit to her king's burdensome request. "How will I ever fulfill this troubling task?" Tree pondered to herself, "without losing the trust and confidence of Adam." She stood alone atop of the silent hill of her mind pondering deeply. Her concentration was averted as she noticed Adam's weary gaze and growing look of concern. Her thoughts fled quickly as tension and nervousness began seep from the depths of her pores. Tree had never felt this uneasy, or tense while in the presence and company of Adam. Today Tree found herself in an awkward position of improv feeling very much reproached by the shameful indigence in harboring ulterior motives.

"Cain," Adam answered, "he is well and has grown since you last set eyes on him" As Adam spoke his eyes were fixed on Tree frame examining over her feeble state with pity, and fear. Adam wanted to ask Tree if she was ill but did not want to seem rude or intrusive to such personal matters. "Anyhow" Adam continued, "it has been long since we had the chance to enjoy each other's company." Tree began to feel a whim of relief as she began to engage and absorb the kindling warmth and energy of Adam's kindness and friendship. Tree attempted feverishly to conjure up a delectable fruit from her frail limbs for Adams enjoyment. She flushed with shame and embarrassment after discovering that she could not host or produce an adequate fruit for her visitor. Noticing her struggling attempt Adam inquired upon her health. "Is everything well with you Tree?" The simple question appeared to upset Tree sending her into an emotional whirlwind. Adams thoughtful inquiry though innocuous somehow managed to trigger Tree drawing tense feelings, and emotions that she attempted to suppress. She tried to retain her composure and save face meeting Adam's inquiry with a smile and nervous laughter. "Oh, yes, don't be foolish, why of course..." All the while straining desperately to produce a sizable fruit to serve and feed her guest.

After some effort and struggle Tree managed to yield a small fruit resembling a tangerine of some sorts. The fruit was noticeably small in proportion unlike the fruits that Adam was accustomed to eating. Adam was used to seeing larger sized oranges and fruits speckled about Tree's branches like decorative ornaments in her hair. Adam was baffled as to the name of the petite size fruit; however, his hunger and appetite would not refuse or turn away the kind gesture. Adam peeled back the strange fruit and began feasting away at the savory morsel. The ripened fruit was sweet and tarty however tasted much better than the larger sized orange fruits. Adam thanked Tree and perched down into his favorite spot near base of her trunk. Adam chewed slowly almost relishing the taste of the delicious fruits. He peeled away another layer from the fruit and devoured the remaining morsel in the silent company of his dear friend.

Tree appeared nervous shooting glances back and forth at Adam. Her mind and heart both raced with phenomenal speed. She was becoming acutely aware of her strange conduct and behavior. Tree was deeply engrossed in arbitration and council within her private thoughts. She pondered to herself contemplating from a space of sheer desperation. Tree was now searching for the perfect moment and opportunity to unload the weight of her burdens off her shoulders. She felt rather anxious and unsettled in Adams presence. Tree was compromised by the fact that her very life and existence was dependent on Adams kindness and generosity in reception to her request.

The moment between the two friends seemed strangely odd. The looming air of silence that lingered hovering over the pair seemed vague and distant. Adam ate in silence nibbling small bites of the sweet fruit still unsure as to how he would voice his concern without appearing intrusive and causing offense. Tree on the other hand was busy attempting to manage the internal crisis occurring throughout her mind and body. She attempted to regain her composure by trying to settle down her thoughts and calm her nerves. Tree was on edge nursing feelings of tension and uneasiness in her demeanor. She wanted nothing more than to break through the thick air of awkwardness and end the formalities to pose the burning question. However, despite the tension and swelling anxiety, Tree could not find the voice or spirit to speak out and thus missed the mark and opportunity to expel her truth. The mixture of spiraling emotions caused Tree to feel somewhat nauseous. She appeared unable to stomach her implication in the foul act of deceit.

Tree questioned the authenticity of her own voice and scrutinized every chance and opportunity to make her appeal. The practice of over-thinking ultimately caused Tree to remain silent and void of words. Tree stood stoically frozen almost paralyzed by trafficking thoughts racing around in her mind. Adam sat near enough to Tree that he could hear the thumping sound of her beating heart. Adam quickly recognized the familiar pattern of thumping noise; however, he was confused as to why Tree's heart pounded so loudly. Adam sat unfazed as though ignorant to the beating of Tree's racing heart. He pretended to be unaffected by the vital sound of life thumping around him. He managed to keep his attention fixed on finishing off the remainder of orange fruit. From his hands and into his mouth Adam devoured the last the delicious morsel. Tree watched Adam in quiet state of tranquility. She observed his calm demeanor, and relaxed attitude which somehow helped to ease tension and evoke reassurance within her. The negative thoughts which rico-cheted back and forth through her mind seem to dissipate instantly. Like an enchanted awakening from a dormant spell, Tree began to dis-pel the intrusive narrative that allowed for fear and shame to fester and flourish in her mind.

Tree prepared herself to speak out and waited for the opportune mo-ment; the perfect segue of some sorts to present her current dilemma. The moment of silence dragged on for what seemed like an eternity for Tree. She was unable to bare the inaudible weight of discomfort for much longer. But before Tree could speak out Adam broke the air of silence surrounding them. "We are making preparations for an-other child." Adam casually mumbled while still chewing his food. The shocking report surprised Tree who was quickly taken aback recalling the prophetic words of her king. She remembered her masters warning foreshadowing the chaos and destruction that would ensue from Adam's descendants. Ordinarily the fortunate news would be cele-brated, but today Tree was weary with suspicion regarding the sudden announcement especially after receiving the king's message.

Tree felt emotionally conflicted regarding the hopeful news however appeared unbiased in the matter. She responded appropriately offering somewhat of a fictitious and fraudulent smile. "Congratulations" Tree announced, cheering halfheartedly. Adam seemed unconvinced though he mirrored Tree's smile returning the same counterfeit grin, and a nervous chuckle as he corrected his friend "Thank you for your generosity, Tree, though the offer is premature." Adam responded cordially "I have yet to act on the matter, and often times find myself paralyzed with fear at the thought of bringing another life and child into this forsaken and barren world." The fragility in Adams voice retained a sad undertone which hinted at his insecurities surrounding childbirth.

"I am betwixt, and confused," Adam confessed suddenly, "my mate wants desperately for us to conceive another child, while I on the other hand am pleased if not content with the present composition and size of our family." Adam suddenly paused as if patiently waiting for Tree's unsolicited response. But before she could interject, or comment Adam furthered on. "I do not see the need for us to rush into such tepid and murky waters especially, considering the severe sickness and affliction suffered during the initial childbirth." Adam looked up at Tree and thanked her again for her support and assistance during the critical episode, acknowledging and stating openly that without her help they would never have made it through.

"No need to thank me," Tree declared, "we are family. I imagine you would do the same for me." "Why, of course." Adam responded with little hesitation. The stage was beginning set for Tree. The perfect scene and opportunity had been placed before her to further the topic and subject of generosity. It was the inconspicuous segue necessary to lead discourse and dialogue; the perfect stage and platform to plead her request. "Tree, can I share something with you." Adam asked preparing to speak openly. "Without judgment, frowns or beaten brows." Tree responded earnestly with a joking smile. "Though my brows may be weary, I will attempt to contain them as well as my judgement." Adam was pleased with Tree's response and at hearing her consent he continued.

"I believe that my beloved finds true value and joy in the practice of fertility, and child rearing. My mate appears to be highly vested in repeating the experience of motherhood." Adam rested his head comfortably against Tree's side before expelling a heavy sigh of exhaustion. "Children bring happiness into our lives," Adam admitted, "they fulfill within us a void, and emptiness, that only the heavens can attest. Children offer new perspectives to our very existence adding substance to our lives. I find the stock of my appraisal and worth to greatly overvalued in the gleaming eyes of my proud son. Cain helped me to discover the passion and fulfillment of joy redefining the terms of intimacy, affection, and love. The blissful sound of a child's laughter cannot be measured or described with simple words."

Tree seemed intrigued by Adams descriptive comparison. His admissions unknowingly described the sustainable power of love serving as powerful power energy sources. Adam continued uninterrupted, "To have a life that is entirely dependent and reliant on you, and your mentorship is an experience like none other..." Adam paused briefly in consideration and reflection of his own words. He raised his head up smiling at Tree. "You of all creatures would understand....", Adam looked up suddenly to discover that another ripened fruit had suddenly appeared. Adam stood up and reached out to pluck the fresh fruit off Tree's lanky limbs.

Adam's gentle and kind words moved Tree immensely, helping to release her from the shackles of her inhibitions. The fact that Adam was able to remember the tireless efforts of her guardianship as a child served to ease tension and stifle concerns. Adam had reaffirmed the importance, and significance of their bond and friendship. In Adam's eyes Tree was the only matriarch he had ever known. She was the only creature with whom he felt safe to share and confide his deepest thoughts and secrets. Tree was empathetic to the fact that Adam grew up isolated and alone. Tree looked on at Adam with the tender eyes of a caring mother. She shared her observations in a way that only a loving mother could surmise. "I understand the root of your troubles" Tree assured Adam. "Your mate desires to erect sturdy, and solid pillars to which the foundation of your legacy can firmly rest upon." Adam was receptive and nodded in agreement. "However, you fear or rather feel unprepared to embark once again on dutiful path of risk and responsibility assigned as a caretaker, and provider." Adam stop peeling the fruit and quickly sat up to listen to Tree as if still processing her words. He marinated for a silent moment and without a word Adam suddenly broke out into laughter.

What started out as snickering gradually increased to moderate chuckles. Building in momentum until finally erupting into bellowing laughter. Adam was simply floored and began rolling on the ground with laughter and tears streaming across his face. Tree, however, was not amused she appeared terribly irritated by Adam's childish and crass behavior. The look of annoyance showed on her face. Adam could plainly see that Tree was not pleased or amused by his humorless antics and stopped. He offered an embarrassing, and subtle apology for his outburst as he sat back down. Adam scarcely realized that he was still wearing the crescent shape smirk over his face and was failing terribly at disguising his amusement. "Please tell me Adam," replied Tree sounding somewhat annoyed and confused. "What is the cause and source of your amusement?" "I am truly sorry," Adam apologized. "Please forgive me as I do not mean to laugh or cause any offense. "I find myself mesmerized with muse by your poetic use of words to paraphrase and surmise the predicament of my current circumstance." Tree looked on at Adam queerly staring as though still baffled by his explanation. "You are absolutely correct," Adam admitted openly "I was laughing at the irony of the situation. I admire the way in which your soothing words have helped to ease my nagging fears and insecurities. As you are aware, my mate was made mute and does not speak or communicate as clearly or eloquently as yourself."

Tree unknowingly blushed at the flattering compliments in which Adam bestowed on her. "Had my mate the ability to speak to me with the mention of "pillars," and "foundations" I would be less troubled and drawn to embark on such radicle endeavors." Tree felt terrible for having accused Adam of mockery especially after dispelling his domestic troubles. It was strange to think as to why God had yet to release Adam's mate from the grips of his inaudible spell. It was apparent that the removal of the creature's voice only helped to further complicate and constrain Adam's relationship with his partner. A binding thought suddenly dawned over Tree imagining the company of silence that Adam endured in his home. If unable to clearly communicate, or understand his mates needs and desires their love would surely wither and perish. "Genius." thought Tree to herself, "masterful; so inspiring, so devious, so ingenious, and yet so simple."

"Tree, I am sorry for laughing..." Adam attempted to apologize, again, but she, would allow it. "No need" Tree answered. "Do not forget, I too, own a sense of humor." Adam returned her smile and continued away at his fruit. He held the wet moist orange in his hand, and just as he was about to take another bite a long and distant memory resurfaced in his mind. "Do you remember?" Adam prompted suddenly. "When I was still a child, and you would tell me, that if I could outrun the lions, and cheetahs out on the fields, I would become the king of their pride. You said that if I could out swim the fishes of the water, I would become lord of every school in the sea. Tree blushed with amusement, at Adam's recalling, "You said to me, that if I could outwit, and outsmart the others, I would become master of my domain and control of my destiny."

Tree scoured her mind to recall the specific childhood story being mentioned "Yes, I remember." Tree confirmed laughing loudly." I remember that particular story being one of your childhood favorites." Adam slowly, nodded in agreement. "May I share a thought?" Tree offered onto Adam, looking down at him. "Why of course.," Adam answered back, "you can always speak openly with me just as I always speak openly with you?" Tree affirmed Adam's response and began to speak openly. "When you were young, you would not sleep; always thinking, and concerning your small mind with the ifs, and why's of the world. Those tales always seemed to bring a calmness over you helping you fall asleep. The innocent stories seemed to cast away your fears and trepidations." Tree was surprised to find that Adam could recall such ancient memories of his childhood. Tree believed that such memories had been erased and forgotten; buried beneath the sands of time amongst the relics of precious moments shared between them.

"I'm sorry Adam if my stories discouraged you in anyway," Tree pleaded gently, "that was not my purpose, nor was it my intention..." "No..." Adam interrupted, his voice strong and firm filled with reassurance. "You misunderstand," Adam continued, "your stories helped me as a child offering me inspiration and hope during my darkest times. And even till this day I still find truth, and wisdom in your telling's and stories." Adam grew anxious as he spoke stammering nervously over his words. He was somewhat tongue tied and staggered nonsensically to regain his nerves and clearly express his thoughts.

Adam drew a deep breath, "I remember your stories," he began again, "had the most profound effect over me. It moved me to act in pursuit of my legacy and greatness. I recall being young and naive at the time when I challenged Cheetah, and Leopard to a lengthy foot race. That day I discovered that I could scarcely keep up with the land animals. At first, I was able to keep pace, however the end mark having been placed far out into the vicinity of the grassland required substantial amount of endurance. I remember running as hard as I could to keep up with Cheetah and Leopard, however my legs would not manage. The two runners sprang swiftly: moving with tenacity and speed. Running behind the two competitors I was forced to shield my face from the trail of dust and debris. I was upset by the loss however my confidence was not utterly shattered by the ordeal of the race.

I decided if I could not win on foot than I would then seize my crown and rightful place in the sparkling waters of the Euphrates rivers.

Once there I challenged the scaly finned creatures of the waters to a friendly sporting match. The exhibition was to include competitive diving and distance racing in symmetrical laps." "Tree!" Adam stopped suddenly peering directly into the face of his captive audience. "I swam ferociously and fared well against some of the native ocean dwellers. However, no matter how hard I pushed myself I could never find the breath or air to stay down long enough to win against those sea creatures.

I nearly drowned attempting to challenge the aquatics beings of the water. I was embarrassed and outright upset with the outcome. Like my race with Cheetah and Leopard, I found myself chastising the fish creatures for setting the goal too close. My battered pride and swelling ego suggested that we further expand the distance. I can admit to it now that it was not the smartest of ideas. However, I was determined to make my mark and prove my point." "Which was?" Tree inquired. "I can't say that I remember." Adam, laughed. "But it was important at the time. I dove into the water and immediately found it difficult to stay afloat. I kicked my legs and arms struggling to swim and compete with the others. This time however I could hardly keep up with them. My tired arms began to grow painfully sore as were my legs. Suddenly, my joints stiffened and cramped from the excessive paddling. The pain was simply unbearable. I could no longer find the strength to kick my feet anymore and began to slowly sink into the water. I nearly drowned had it not been for Dolphin and his school friends who saved me and brought me back to land. My legs and arms felt painfully tender. I managed to humiliate and embarrass myself once again in front of the land and sea animals. Somehow thru that experience I received notoriety and recognition for my brazen courage and audaciousness. I would later receive several invitations and offers to return to compete and race again however, I humbly declined. I realized that it was useless to challenge fishes to swimming competitions and expect to win. The water was an unfavorable arena for me offering minimal advantages. It was then that I realized and accepted that the creatures of land and sea would never allow me to be their king or accept me as their lord and master.

My greatest challenge was yet to come or regrettably rather it never came. This was because I was still upset and filled disappointed for my shortcomings and failures. I was deeply discouraged by my inability to outrun, and out-swim the creatures of Eden that I postponed my aspirations. I strongly detested the taste of defeat and failure which stained my tongue and tastebuds. I gave up and quit that day. I refused to entertain any discussion which involved the subject or mention of my proclaimed destiny. I accepted failure as my fate never giving much thought to the third challenge of outwitting the world and trailing my own path and destiny. Why should I try or attempt to go out into the world when I have already failed, twice before. These thoughts, and more plagued my mind but I was young then and even when shying away from childhood I still thought of myself as being far too small to outwit a single creature let alone outsmart an entire kingdom.

My world no longer seemed vast, I became filled with despair and uncertainty I grew obsessively fearful of failure and disappointment to the point I avoided life's challenges. This decision only helped to stunt my growth and dim my ambitions of achieving greatness. I accepted and associated the idea of not trying with never failing. I happily accepted my carefree existence within the safe confines of Eden's high walls. I lived my life like a delightful daydreamer sheltered from the wrath of misfortune, and failure. I never imagined that one day I would come to live on the other side of those grand walls. However, this strange and foreign world has challenged my childish ideology of not trying and never failing. Life is different here outside of Eden where there is no room for the childish thinking. The mantra of these lands declares that if you do not try, then you are doomed to die." "Try or die", Tree surmised with lightheartedness or laughter as though amused by Adam's telling. "I'm sorry." Tree offered another apology. "Please continue."

"Throughout this experience I have but one regret. that is, I never gave much thought to the potential of my destiny. I never tried to outwit the world or placed much thought or conviction in using my mind to leverage my handicap and make up for my shortcomings. I never should have given up so easily in pursuing my childhood quest. I should have relied more on my intellect to help achieve my goal and purpose. I believe now I could have won and garnered the admiration and respect of Eden residents without threat or the use of physical force. It is not my intention to boast, but I have come to the realization that I am unlike any creature roaming this world. Mark my words Tree, man is keen, and obsessive by nature. My mind has the supernatural ability to imagine and resolve problems and challenges while exploring variations of possible outcomes." "Wow, that sounds remarkable" Tree responded, eager to learn more of Adam abilities.

"Yes." Adam agreed "Had I continued the path and pursuit of greatness I would have figured a way to challenge and champion those land and water creatures. Had applied as much wit and intellect to overcoming obstacle rather than relying on physical strength alone. I am confident that I would have figured out a way to overcome the physical barriers and challenges which I regarded as obstacles. I am sure that by now I would have figured out a way to win and achieved my intended purpose. Rather than running away from adversity I should have stood firm and learned to face failure and defeat as teachable moments and experiences. But I was young then, still inexperienced at navigating difficult terrains of life. I was never taught how to circumnavigate and regulate the charge of emotions that surged within me. And had I given myself grace and allowed for time and space to meditate. I would have surely discovered an alternative way to outrun and best Leopard, and Cheetah in a race. I never gave enough thought to the possible ways in which I could learn to outswim and outmaneuver the agile and elusive and creatures of the water."

An indistinguishable look of sadness fell on the face and spirit as Adam concluded his story. "But I know better now. " Adam smiled nodding agreeably, "I have already begun to instill within Cain the significant value of harnessing wit and intellect. Conventional wisdom and life have profoundly revealed to me the indisputable truth that one can never fail, if one never gives up. No matter how big or lofty the dream, or how ambitious the pursuit of one's goal. Persistence and grit many times can unlock obstacles and remove barriers and challenges faced. This gem and nugget of truth I plan to pass on to all my children and descendants to never stop trying. Man will never give up!" Adam declared proudly.

Tree was very much moved by Adams admission and telling revelation. At the time she had no idea that her stories made such an impactful impression on Adam's childhood. Tree's tales would become the fuel and gas which would propel Adam dreams and ambitions forward. Tree had little awareness of the discord and inner turmoil that Adam harbored surrounding his harsh treatment and dismissal from the garden. Adam had never spoken or expressed out loud to Tree his seeded resentment and harbored feelings of contempt for having been barred from Eden and stripped of his royal birthright. Tree was aware and understood very well Adam's prescribed destiny which was to reign supreme over this world and the heavens as God originally intended. Tree felt provoked somewhat fraught with considerable remorse in realizing that she had failed to explore Adam feelings surrounding his own ambitions and hopes.

Tree's pride, and happiness began to morph into emotions of shame, and guilt. She felt terrible for having driven Adam into such a frenzied and misguided state of belief. Adam held the misguided belief that he alone could charter the course of his path and destiny. "I should have told him the truth," Tree regretted, "while he was still young, but instead I told him stories, of outrunning wild beasts, and sea creatures." Tree felt a sense of disappointed reflecting over her historic endeavors .She appeared consumed with remorse and wanted nothing more than to correct the errors of her past by speaking openly.

"Adam," Tree called out, "you are no longer a child. You have grown to become a great being. You are a creature of unspeakable potential, and possibilities. Your uniqueness is your true strength, and power. It is true that our lord and master gave us shape, and design, but you stand before me in rare likeness of our king. Not just in resemblance and image but in tenacity and breadth. You have managed to somehow breach the realms of conception to become a mighty creator yourself, have you not? You and your mate have somehow managed to forge life and create a being of your own. And just as his father before him Cain, will possess a similar appetite and energetic outlook on his path and search for purpose and meaning. I imagine that Cain will grow up to master everything that he sees or touches. Anything that draws his interest or attracts his senses will be subject to his will to do with as he wishes." Adam smiled nervously at never having considered the potential elevation and plight of his son. "Please Adam, promise me," Tree began to plea, "that no matter what happens on your journey that you will never forget who you are and where you came from. As you may already know this unflattering world will attempt to discount and minimize your value. The weight and pressures of this world will attempt to crush and bend your royal crown however, you must never allow it to break. The world will try to soil and sully your good name and reputation, but you must never allow those stains to change you. This world will attempt to deny you your rightful place and criticize your every choice and indecisions. Despite your circumstances do not forget that you are still precious and valuable. You are righteously refined and rightfully inclined to stand as nobility; deserving of the honor and title of prince." The truth of Tree's wisdom was undeniable. The humbling weight or her words caused Adam to lower his head in obedience nodding silently in agreement.

At that moment the world seemed to slow down for the two. The quiet stillness eventually drew some tension and uneasiness between the pair. A putrid scent of resentment was beginning to mask and fill the air them. The strange odor of uneasiness lingered between the couple like a foul stench irritating their senses. It was as though something was unspoken and being neglected between the two. The fumes of awkwardness began to slowly subside, and fade carried away by the winds. The bright rays of the sun suddenly appeared. The large clouds that hovered across the vast blue sky dispersed leaving the visibly large sun to shine and illuminate the sky. The fiery star shone bright from high above beaming down heat, and warmth over the already dry and barren lands. Tree's frail limbs could not offer Adam any shade or give him refuge to escape the wrath of the sweltering sun.

It did not take long before Adam became parched and overcome with fatigue. Adam was acutely attuned with his bodily needs and understood that the weary moment called for rest. His decision to rest was not at all surprising as it aligned perfectly in synch with his usual midday nap time. Adam perched his tired head against Tree's large body and nestled himself opposite the direction of the sun. Sitting comfortably, Adam gave out a howling yawn. "Tree," Adam called out. "Seriously, was I a good child?" He inquired in an infused juvenile tone. Tree paused for a moment to analyze his question, and with some uncertainty she replied, "By good, what do you mean Adam?" Tree, answered. Adam was tired, and nearly half asleep. His eyes were closed as he responded. "I mean did I bring you joy, and bliss" he yawned once again. His fatigued and tired mind quickly rephrased the question. "Did I bring meaning and purpose to your life, the... way... Cain fills...mine..." Adam stopped suddenly. "Why, yes." Tree confessed openly heartedly. "You have brought more joy to my life than ever intended in my design. You are my beloved Adam the only creature who can do no wrong in my eyes." Despite her thoughtful remark it was too late. Adam had already fallen fast asleep like a slumbering child along his mother side. This however did not discourage or detour Tree as she continued carrying on.

"It was your smile," Tree answered in a quiet whisper, "which first snagged my heart and disarmed me." Tree playfully attempted to mimic the smile which cemented their bond, and friendship. "At the time your small face and huge smile shinning bright like a burning star drew warmth over my body and heart..." The moment seemed all too perfect as Tree's energy of her spirit began to slowly return to her body. In absence of anxiety and fear filled thoughts Tree's frail and ailing body was beginning to show signs of improvement. As a response to Adams affection and love Tree body began to swell morbidly. The very girth of her frame expanded beyond the bounds of its original plot and state. "I was intrigued if not entranced by our introduction," Tree continued with her admission all but unaware as to the transformation that was taking place. "I admit when I first met you and saw those radiantly soft eyes I was immediately enamored and stricken with infatuation only moments after meeting you…" The colors of her leaves slowly transitioned changing from brittle copper back to a fluorescent hue of green. A sigh of relief came over Tree feeling compelled to sing a sweet hymn. The olden lullaby was a hymn which Adam had not heard since his early childhood.

The harmony of Tree's voice against the ruffling crescendo of her leafy hair produced the perfect euphony of sounds. And though Adam's eyes were closed shut, his ears were still open to hearing his favorite opera singer perform. Adam immediately recognized the sentimental piece being performed and attempted desperately to pry open to view the performance. Despite his efforts, Adam was much too tired and overcome with exhaustion to open his eyes. He was unable to lift the weary weight of sleep and fatigue from over his brows. The slow tune of Tree's voice only helped to assist Adam to fall safely back into the nether realms of sleep. While in the unconscious state Adam dreamt himself home again living in the carefree environment and paradise of Eden. The nostalgic tune had not been heard by Adam since his early days. It was understandable that his subconscious would transport him to a familiar setting and place in his mind. Adams decision to return to the garden was undoubtedly provoked by the signature sound of his favorite song.

It was nearly dawn when Adam awoke to from his slumber. He had slept much longer than intended and began stir. He sprang up to his fee suddenly after realizing that he was not home. "Oh my…" Adam remarked after awakening from his tenacious nap. "What hour is it?" he inquired frantically, "I must return home without haste," Adam announced with sense of urgency. "My family must be terribly worried if not concerned regarding my whereabouts" "I agree" said Tree "it is rather late, but before you go, I must ask one favor from you. It is a strange request to beset upon you but none the less I will ask of it still." A strange emotion dawned over Tree as she strained to speak, "I would like you to bring me a lock of your mates' hair." Tree surrendered in a nimble voice as if unconvinced by the warrant of her own request. Adam looked at Tree rather queerly and mirrored the same qualifying sentiments. He too was very much puzzled by the odd request. "You want a locket of my mates' hair?" He repeated, hoping to add clarity to confusion.

The strange emotions soon formed into a weary nervousness. Tree could feel the heavy backlash of her strange request. "Well yes." She intuitively confirmed. "The lock of hair is..." Tree ransacked her mind for a plausible excuse or reason as to why she a Tree of all things would need with a lock of hair. "...So that, I may beg, his highness to create a companion.... for me." Tree witfully added. "One to keep me company and provide me engagement for as you can see..." Looking down at the number of fallen limbs, and branches on the ground. "I often times become lonely, especially here in the desolate outskirts" Tree hid her face from Adam feeling somewhat ashamed by the fictional act of her performance. She drew her gaze upward at the dimming sky to marvel over the twinkling stars. Tree could not find the strength to look Adam in his eyes and as a result she evaded his gaze. She kept her face plastered to the sky staring upward into the darkness of the dwindling night.

The burden of guilt, and shame which stacked like heavy weights over Tree's conscious began to force her gaze downward into Adams direction. Tree was gripped with paranoia and burdened with intrusive thoughts invading her subconscious and taunting her insecurities. She felt as transparent as glass believing that Adam could see directly thru her falsehood. Tree was certain that Adam would challenge if not expose her poorly concealed attempt at lying. Her mind raced with endless possibilities conjuring up various ways in which the awkward scene would play out. She braced herself imagining the worst-case scenario and outcome concluding with a dramatic refusal of Adams support. Her face softened with dew. Tree appeared flustered and flushed; her nerves raced violently. "Had I made my proposal earlier in the day Adam may never have picked up or taken notice of the subtle signs and clues exposing my nervousness. By this point Tree was growing anxious and desperate for a response. Any answer would have sufficed to ease the climax of tension and anxiety surrounding Tree as she waited for Adam to respond.

Tree seemed critical of the deceptive act and was somewhat anxious and uneasy with the thought of abating and misdirecting truth. "I cannot take this silence any longer," Tree shouted to herself growing rather annoyed by the linger of silence. What seem to drag on for an eternity in Tree's mind lasted but a few seconds or so in reality. "What will be his answer?" Tree pondered repeatedly to herself and was growing impatient for Adam to answer. Tree felt consumed with guilt, she was unprepared to manage the surge of emotions racing through her body. It was safe to believe that at any moment Tree would explode from the buildup of pressure and tension. Tree felt as though she was not designed to tell lies or withhold truths. The entire ordeal appeared morally taxing and overwhelmingly for Tree to manage.

Adam who was growing close if not ready to take his leave had yet to give an answer to the request. In observing his hesitation Tree began to accept the thought of defeat and considered whether to leverage her appeal by offering to disclose and reveal the truths behind her strange request. Tree was growing more nervous and frantic in her thoughts. She considered the punitive retaliation for her treachery for having divulged or shared her master words. Such a confession would ultimately result in the termination and end of her service to the king. Tree understood that the ramifications of her decision would jeopardize and risk her own life at the expense and cost of betrayal and treachery. Tree was tired of cowering beneath her master thumb and rule. She was beginning to grow repugnantly indifferent to the concept of life and death.

Tree was growing comfortable with accepting her end and demise. The fiery embers of her emotion's began to stoke uncontrollably in response to the absence of fear. Tree felt overwhelmingly torn and desperate to be absolved of both treason and betrayal. She refused to allow the wrath of God to impede and detour her from unveiling the truth. Feeling exhausted Tree gave a hefty sigh. "This is truly cruel and unusual punishment." She thought to herself no longer willing to wait. Just as Tree was gathering her nerves to speak out, if not a moment sooner before she could utter a sound Adam answered. "Alright, Tree, I will do it." Tree was surprised if not relieved by the exact timing of Adam's response. "Wait, are sure certain?" Tree inquired, as if somewhat still astonished, and unclear as to whether Adam's reply was an illusion or daydream.

"A simple lock of hair," Adam answered, "is but a minor fee to pay; nearly insignificant in comparison to the large debt of gratitude owed." Adam stood firm placing his palms directly on Tree, "I owe you so much more for having nurtured me kept me safe at every expense and cost to yourself. Adams eyes began to dampen as he spoke, right along with Tree whose watery eyes were already swelling with moist tears. "My debt to you is irredeemable worth much more than a lock of hair could ever repay." Adam bowed gently placing his head against Tree face, "I do not know anyone more deserving of companionship than yourself. We shall make it so that you are never feel alone again."

Tree began to sob uncontrollably at Adams ballad conflicted mostly by the dueling turmoil and internal conflict. "My time here draws late," Adam declared, "I must take leave now for darkness will soon be upon us." Adam turned to walk away, "I will return soon enough my dear friend." Adam shouted from a distance and began treading quickly scurrying through the night. Adam ran off into the distance, galloping towards the horizon trailing home in his usual path. It was not long before Adam became a faint image resembling that of a silhouette beneath glowing moonlight.

Tree eyes followed Adam into the distance looking on as far she could until finally losing sight of him. When no longer able to view Adam in the proximity Tree turned her attention and gaze upward looking up at the blanketed sky, taking special notice to the splatter of newly lit stars. Drawing special attention to the moon Tree, observed how oddly bright the candescent the moon appeared to glow on this specific night. The crescent moon resembled a sly smirk that seemed to irritate and taunt her as she projected her feelings and insecurities outwardly towards the universe. Tree was without a doubt convinced the counterfeit smile was indeed the indistinguishable smirk of God. She drew suspicion for a moment but quickly dismissed her assumptions as ridiculous. Tree rejoiced and was fueled with excitement enthralled by the amicable gesture of her benevolent friend. Adam's sincere and kind words were truly moving, and had it not been for the lie that seemed to prick and irritate Tree's mind the day would have been perfectly blissful.

11

The Reckoning

An ample amount of time had gone by since Adam had last seen his beloved friend. He had intended to visit Tree sooner but was rather consumed with managing domestic affairs in his home. Adam's mate was once again with child, brimming past the early stages of fertility. His boy Cain was bed-bound after an incident in which the young lad sprained his foot while out hunting with his father. Adam had his hands full caring for his family. He kept himself employed and busy working to find and gather food and nourishment for his growing family.

Adam understood very well that this birth would be especially difficult for them to endure recalling the challenges experienced during Cains birth and his passage into life. Adam was thankful for Tree and accredited her for assisting and supporting him through those challenging times. The family were no longer receiving nutritional aide or support from Tree since her return to Eden. Adam could no longer access to the bountiful selection of her fruits and produce as freely as before. Many times, during the day Adams mind would drift off into a fantasy world. He often entertained himself with thoughtful possibilities of what life would be like for him in Eden. Adam imagined how much simpler and better off his family and life would be if they all resided and lived in Eden surrounded by bountiful fields and delectables pleasures. It was undeniably true that the conditions of the garden were much more suitable of a place and settlement than the desolate outskirts. The paradise offered safety and nourishment making the fear of starvation the least of the family's worries. Eden was an observable contrast to the stoney concrete world. The unfertile land outside of Eden was barren and absent of exotic fruits and crops. It substituted fruits and berries in exchange for wild game and creatures of prey.

These were hard times for Adam and his family. The departure of Tree left Adams family with a supplemental sense emptiness. Her tasty fruits were no longer accessible to the family. The savage creatures and beast that served as prey and wild game which Adam frequently hunted began to dwindle and gradually decline. Adam blamed himself for the conflict and shortage viewing it as result of his own conjuring and doing. It was true that Adam's growing reputation as a skilled hunter and scavenger was becoming fearfully renowned and regarded throughout in the wilderness. Adam and Cain had become remarkable hunters who worked together to take down beasts of gargantuan, and colossal sizes. The beasts and creature of the wild came to know of and fear the dangerous duo. The saw man as being savage predators that menacingly hunted down and slayed any creature that dared to loiter or leer near their path or proximity.

The beasts that were fortunate enough to spot the stealthy hunters were able to run away narrowly escaping with their lives. Adam and Cain exercised precision, and tact in homing their skills each taking personal pride in their unique hunting style and technique. They minimized the outcome of failure as often as possible and saw to it that the creatures with whom they prayed upon did not escape or shriek loudly to startle of alarm the herd of others. Their failed attempts though seldom often resulted in fluttering outcries and darting retreat of their would-be victim. The escape served as a deterrent signaling danger to other potential prey. This often resulted in stampede of creatures fleeing to escape danger believing that man was undoubtedly within the vicinity. Adam and Cain witnessed the cascade of events led by a single wild beast who managed to cleverly escape and ran off screaming hysterically. The fearful beast instantly incited fear and panic provoking the other creatures to run off as well. The creatures ran instinctively blinded by their innate sense of fear. They sought to escape unforeseen dangers weary to the thought of impending doom. The distance and range of their retreat was becoming problematic as the creatures began to recede further out into the barren open lands. The herd of savage creatures were unlikely to return to the same location. Many of the savage creatures opted to relocate for their own safety. The traveled further into the foreign and unventured grounds. The migration which furthered the creature's distance ultimately increased the duration of their hunt. The duration of their efforts consisted mostly of traveling time. Adam and Cain were becoming forced regularly to travel further, and further out in search of nutrition and sustenance. They found themselves chasing after creatures into new territory and grazing grounds.

Usually the distance, and time went unnoticed, while in the company of his son, but since Cains accident Adam found himself traveling alone more frequently. Even though the boy begged his father to accompany him on his journey Adam refused believing that the long distance would only worsen the condition of his foot and hinder his recovery. Cain was sad to see his father leave early mornings unaccompanied and unaided. He did his part in assisting his father to prepare for the day by sharpening and cleaning Adams tools organizing and placing them into a large satchel and duffle sack designed by his mother. The nifty satchel was crafted with a sturdy latch buckle so that Adam could wear the bag on his shoulders or over his back to avoid being bombarded and pierced by the sharp instruments.

On this day Adam was unlucky in finding any beastly creatures in the wilderness. He surveyed the area numerous times but was unable to find a single beast to hunt down and slay. It was as though the savage beasts were expecting his arrival and took the precautionary effort to distance themselves from their usual grazing grounds. Adam traveled the deserted path in direction of the backwaters. He hoped the combination of the heat and dry air had brought the creatures to the river to drink and quench their thirst. He walked beneath the blazing sun until finally he arrived at the riverbank where he discovered the area largely crowded. Many of the missing creatures were found idling around the riverbank.

Some of the creatures were engrossed in drink, while others bathed in the cool water. The larger of the creatures stood opposite their prey. A sense of neutrality surrounded the drinking area. There was, an unspoken sense of peace that fell over the small area. The unsuspecting congregation of creatures gathered peacefully. They were unaware of the potential danger and stalking presence lurking over them.

Adam hid behind a large boulder away from the view of his unsuspecting prey. He concealed himself to avoid drawing any attention from the cluster wild beasts. His discovery would only help to send the creatures fleeing in panicked state. Or worse they would all unite and work together to chase him off and drive him away. Adam wasted little time rummaging through his sack in search for the perfect weapon or appropriate tool that would serve him in range and distance. He retrieved from his sack a leathery belt and two dense rocks with jagged edges. He planned to use to the rock to strike down and disable the wild prey.

Adam decided that the sling was the appropriate tool to serve him in range and distance. He intended to strike down one of the larger sized creatures with a fierce fling of his sling. Adam was more than aware of the fatal impact and dangerous capabilities of the simple yet powerful sling. A hard blow to the temple and head could easily cause a concussion or worse render its victim lifeless. Adam slowly stepped forward into the light away from the cloak of the shadowy boulder. He surveyed the area until finally he spotted the perfect victim standing alone and away from the others. He imagined that it would be a hasty and quiet kill; one that would allow him to quietly swoop in and retrieve the fallen creature. Adam believed he possessed the stealthy and agility to complete the task all without being noticed or arousing the suspicion of the others.

With little time for hesitation Adam began by placing one of the densely sharp rocks into the cusp of the sling and began twirling the rock over his head. The sling sung a humming tune that soon developed into a loud wailing cry whistling louder with every rotation. It was not long before the shrieking war cry of Adams sling was heard cutting rapidly through the air in perpetual motion. Set on his target Adam marked the unsuspecting prey for death and steadied his aim as he prepared to release sling. Adam took comfort in the belief that if even if he missed his mark in aiming for creature's head. He was certain that the intense force of the rock would undoubtedly wound and disarm the creature long enough for him restock a second rock into his sling to deliver the final blow and seal the creature's fate.

Adam drew forth intently focused on the precise calculation of his path and trajectory. He measured the range along with distance and how much inertia and strength would be needed to send the rock in direction of its target. Adam inched closer stealthily moving carefully without breaking concentration or losing sight of his victim. Now Adams only fear was that of being spotted or discovered by a malingering onlooker within the crowd. He understood well the chaos and disruption that would instantly ensue if any of the creatures discovered him lurking amongst the herd of ravenous creatures.

The unsuspecting beasts grazed about freely without the slightest idea that in mere moments one of them would fall victim to the hands of man. Adam mustered strength in his arm his wailing sling whistling loudly through the air. He stepped forth to send the rock flying however Adam did not bother to look down or take notice of the large pile of manure lying on the ground. "Ahhh!" Adam hollered with an alarming cry. He reacted erratically to having stepped foot first into moist dung. He lost his footing in his concentration and prematurely discharged both the rock and sling from his grips. Adam recovered quickly but could not account as to the exact coarse and direction of his rock had sling. The element of surprise which served to be advantageous to Adam was now lost as his presence and location were now revealed to the public.

The echoing sound of Adams outcry served as cause for alarm amongst the wild and distant creatures. The unfamiliar noise captured the attention and curiosity of the brooding creatures as they searched around them. They darted their eyes back and forth searching about wearing baffled looks of confusion on their faces. The lost rock which Adam accidently flung into the air soared high up before crashing suddenly into the peaceful still waters. The velocity and impact caused an eruption of water to shoot upward splashing the faces of some frightened and unsuspecting creatures. They reacted unamused and appeared rather annoyed by the disturbance. It did not take the beasts very long to accept their inclinations that man was present somewhere in the vicinity scouring nearby. The very thought of man's presence produced panic and fear amongst the wild beasts understanding very well man's affinity for hunting and expertise in taking down prey. The hurling rock crashing suddenly into the water served as an indication and warning of potential danger. They observed the failed attempt against their lives with radicle contempt and trepidation. These negative feelings soon developed into feelings of fear and panic amongst the surrounding creatures. Reacting impulsively and without regard several beastly creatures began fleeing and scurrying away. They were proactive in their anxiety very much impatient to wait for visual confirmation of man. The desperate act provoked other creatures to react accordingly and join the stampeding march of frightened creatures. They moved swiftly while still afforded the opportunity to escape.

In their frantic retreat the creatures scurried about splashing wildly in effort to exit the murky water. The savage beasts charged on violently relentless and disorganized in their attempt to flee and escape the scene. It wasn't long before the entire riverbank was empty with all the wild creatures having fled and vacated the area. Adam found himself standing alone upset and annoyed by the mishap of missing his mark. The onset of frustration dawned over Adam in realization that he would not be able to bring home a meal for his family on this day. It was times like these when Adam felt lowly and filled with disappointment that he would search out support and comfort from his beloved friend. Tree was always there for Adam, ready to offer kind redeeming words that would lift his spirits. Tree was the only creature that could offer nourishment to both his body and mind. Left with nowhere else to turn Adam accepted his defeat and shamefully gathered his tools and other belongings and began his crippling walk. Adam made up his mind that he would venture to Eden to check on the recovery and health of dear friend and seek out her council and wisdom.

Traveling to Eden would be a long and vigorous journey however Adam was prepared to travel and trudge the lengthy expedition. Adam began to walk towards the familiar road and beaten path leading to the grand walls. Adam tread for miles feeling the soreness and ache of every step beneath his feet. He was exhausted however flushed with determination refusing to yield to the pangs and throbbing soreness in his legs. Adam felt as though he was walking aimlessly and entertained on many instances the thought and notion of giving up and simply returning home. He ignored the intrusive thoughts calling for his retreat and return home, Adam demonstrated persistence and perseverance dragging his feeble legs forward until finally arriving at the grand walls.

Adam stood before the small plot of land where Tree once stood. He surveyed the grand wall and upon closer inspection of the barred exterior he observed a doorway. There now stood a large gaping hole breaching inward. The stoney doorway resembled that of a carved entrance and pathway. The funneled walls revealed a hollowed-out pathway and leading directly into Eden. The stoned corridor though shadowy and deep filled Adam with mysticism and enchantment. He was drawn by the aesthetic design and remarkable construction of the marbled pathway. Adam was surprised to find that there was no one assigned to the safeguarding and protecting the sacred doorway. There was no sentinels or doorkeeper to keep out uninvited intruders from waltzing into Eden. Adam stopped concerning himself with Eden's lack of security and proceeded to walk through the dark corridor. He was drawn forth by luminescent light the radiating at the end of the tunnel.

Adam made his way through the enchanted space emerging from the other side of the tunnel into Eden. A sudden look of amazement fell over Adams face as he stood glaring over the scenery. Adam was profoundly mesmerized by the beauty and magnificence of the land. Eden was a wonderland decked and draped in greenery. Inside the garden the air smelled fresher the sky seemed to shine a more radiant hue of blue. Adams extended absence and time outside Eden now made him view his former home much differently. His recollection of the garden had been vastly outdated since he last remembered. Eden was no longer the botanical jungle that he recalled in his youth. The land seemed evolved and somewhat transformed in its appearance. The antiquity of the landscape retained an air of mysticism which seemed to capture if not illustrate the artistic integrity of its grand landscape.

The audit of Adams homecoming was strangely polished with everything appearing perfectly shaped and in order. It was as if the garden was expecting his arrival and made immeasurable efforts to ensure a hospitable experience. Adam strolled through garden aimlessly and could scarcely recognize how immaculately kept and clean the paradise now seemed. He walked about the garden like a tourist surveying strange and unfamiliar land. Every step was met with the sound and voices of animals welcoming Adam back to Eden. Familiar animals that Adam had forgotten, and not seen his youth trotted up to him to greet and welcome him home. Some faces Adam instantly recognized while others he was unable to recollect. The animals of the garden flocked in groves to see if not witness for themselves the legendary man creature.

Deer and her fawn were the first to welcome the prince back to the kingdom. "Welcome home Adam." Deer cheered. "Yes, welcome." Recited a young fawn shadowing behind its mother. "Thank you," Adam, answered back. His kind and gentle demeanor prompted more creatures to approach him. Antelope came next accompanied by Badger, Beaver, and Bear who all came pay their respects to the noble prince. Following behind the others were Coyote, Cheetah. Crow and Raven among other feathery creatures yelled and exchanged pleasantries from high up in sky. A path was of egress was mad for Fox and Elephant as they strolled by idly through the crowd. Strolling behind them was the long necks of

Ostrich and Giraffe carrying Heron and Crane settled comfortably atop their heads. The duo appearing too exhausted to fly and decided it was easier to hitch a ride. Lion, Leopard and Panther made an appearance as well as did ,Tiger, and Zebra. There was a colorful host of wild animals and creatures that showed up to pay homage and celebrate the return of the prince.

The news spread quickly regarding Adam's arrival as more animals came forth to offer greetings. Many of the younger generational creatures arrived with hopes of laying eyes on the legendary man being. The youthful creatures of Eden had never seen Adam or laid eyes on man. In their eyes he was but a legendary character shared in folklore stories told to them by their parents and elders. The young and youthful hurried with eagerness clamoring together in groups to meet and see man. Adam felt a strong sense of admiration and gratitude towards those that gathered around and surrounded him with praise and kind words. The prince as Adam was often referred to by his title of nobility. It was not long before Adam began to revel in the praise and worship he received from the inhabitants. They offered affectionate reconciliation and praise holding firm to the narrative and belief that his presence was sorely missed. Many of his loyal subjects and fans expressed wholeheartedly that his unfair his dismissal and removal from Eden was unconstitutional. They viewed Adams displacement and extended absence as a taxing toll placed over the community. It appeared that Adams banishment from the Eden provoked a sense of sadness and disappointment over the entire kingdom.

Adam continued to look around examining over the landscape searching about for his dear friend Tree but could find her. In the company of his enthusiasts and admirers Adam walked about with a soulful strut that matched the glowing smile over his face. He walked with grace, and ease moving about freely as though already familiar with the homeland. Adam still appeared mesmerized marveling over the gorgeous landscape. The vacuum of his eyes managed to take in the details of the luxurious garden. Adam was now a student of the land studying closely with newly formed sense of astonishment, and amazement. Deep rooted emotions began to resurface for Adam after having deliberately made the decision and choice to forget the splendors of his homeland. Adam was now being confronted with ravishing force and wonderous bounty that Eden had to offer.

Adam looked over the assortment of vibrant flowers noticing the pattern of blossoming colorful which decked the garden landscape. The colorful petals helped to accentuate and more so distinguish the various shades of greenery. The mesmerizing scene was truly picturesque and for a stationary moment Adam lost himself in all Eden's beauty. Adam was enchanted by the fresh fragrance of moist pollen and recalled through his senses treasured moments of his youth. The nostalgic recall felt euphoric for Adam causing an overhaul of sentimental emotions to spill over him. Adam appeared rejoiced as reminisced over memories of when he called the garden his home.

In that moment Adam felt happy and complete. He declared privately that he never wanted to leave the beautiful paradise. Adam only wished that his mate and child could share in the amazing experience. The thought of his partner and son witnessing the massive wonderland of Eden for themselves brought Adam great delight. "Oh, how they would love this place." Adam fantasized for a moment and imagined seeing his family prancing and frolicking through the fields. The image of his family together in Eden brought with it a heartwarming feeling and sensation over Adam. The change of lifestyle would serve favorably to offer relief to his family against the unfavorable conditions of the harsh terrain. Life outside of Eden was barren and bleak in contrast and comparison to the world of Eden. Adam reflected briefly on the circumstances of the outside world viewing it as a dry and desolate wasteland. The barren and empty world outside of Eden produced only dense stones and sharp rocks as its landscape. The malignant environment outside of Eden appeared to Adam as nothing more than a condemned and neglected wasteland where nothing was expected to thrive. When juxtaposed and leveraged against the outside world Eden could easily be viewed as the favorable estate.

Adam was being followed by an entourage of creatures as he toured the land. It was not until he encountered a brightly colored bird fluttering quickly through the air. The agile and swift bird flew downward shuttering its wing near Adam's face. "Do not be startled," reassured the small, winged creature in a sharp finicky voice. "We have been awaiting your arrival." "My arrival." Adam repeated. "But, who are you?" he asked the strange bird. "My apologies your royal prince. I am Hummingbird." Answered the colorful bird politely. "I was sent by Tree to serve as a chaperon and liaison to meet her." "Tree!" Adam repeated after hearing the mention of her name. "Where is Tree?" He pleaded enthusiastically. "Please take me to her." And without another word shared or moment spared Hummingbird flew off and into the air.

"Follow me!" Urged the small bird calling out from high above. Hummingbird fluttered and shifted quickly moving side to side through the air. "I will guide you to Tree." Announced the winged creature moved swiftly through the air" Hummingbird swooped and swaying about effortlessly through the air. Adam ran after the shifty bird attempting desperately to keep within pace of the elusive animal. He tracked after the feathery creature imploring every grain of his being and strength to keep up and maintain sight of the winged creature. The agile bird maneuvered through the sky while Adam gave chase from the ground. Adam ignored the numbing pain which began to swell from his feet. His eyes and attention were narrowly fixed on the bird maneuvering through the canopies of the forest treetops. Adam ran madly through the labyrinth forest directed by eclipsing shadow of winged creature above him. Hummingbird began glide down gently escaping the blinding sun. The slow descent brought the intense chase to an exhaustive halt. Adam was exhausted and plagued with fatigue from endless running. His body and face drenched with sweat and moist droplets. Adams mouth and nostrils flared open to take in and absorb more air into his lungs. He appeared out of breath; panting desperately in attempt to collect air and regain his composure.

Adam clung desperately to his chest inhaling deeply to collect air and breath into his lungs and body. He attempted to express his gratitude to the winged creature for allowing the short intermission and moment of rest. Adam withdrew his gaze from the ground and slowly began to lift his head upward to thank Hummingbird. He paused however, finding himself caught within the throes of distraction. Adam appeared obsessed with the bountiful wonder of vastness and beauty surrounding him. He was surprised to find himself back home standing at the center and heart of Eden where he was brought up and reared as a child.

Subdued by nostalgia confronted with forgotten thoughts and memories of his childhood Adam was confronted with archived images of childhood which he believed had been lost and since forgotten. He began to rejoice and smile happily recalling the familiar scent and sweet aroma of the wildflowers blooming in the fresh meadows. Adam searched the sky for his winged escort and companion friend and found the exhausted bird perched atop a large sturdy branch. It didn't take long for Adam to make the connection and surprising discovery and realization that Hummingbird was sitting comfortably on the limbs belonging to his dearest friend Tree. Eager to confirm his suspicion and rekindle their union he called out ecstatically "Tree!!!" Adam cried out repeatedly rejoicing with uncontainable excitement at the thought of having located her.

12

The Homecoming

Adam called out to Tree but received no response. He examined her body closer taking notice to how healthy and nourished she now appeared. Tree looked fully restored in her natural habitat and rightful place. She no longer appeared disfigured, and decrepit having been returned to her original state and good health. She now stood tall and firmly erect stationed at the heart and center of the garden. In her company Adam observed a shadowy figure lurking around and about peeking out periodically from behind the base of Trees frame and large body. "Hello, Adam," Tree answered awakening to the familiar sound and voice calling out to her. Tree was thrilled with enthusiasm at the sight and sudden appearance of his Adam. "Come forth my dear friend" she called out to him. "Let me take a look at you."

Despite the invitation Adam walked cautiously towards Tree. His gaze was fixed on the strange figure hiding behind his dear friend. "Hello Adam," Tree announced again, "I see you have managed to find your way home." Adam appeared somewhat distracted by the shadowy figure lurking in the background. "The garden has changed much since I last remembered wouldn't you agree?" Adam appeared heightened and alert to the looming stranger present in their company. "Yes," Adam answered inattentively. "It is nice to see you that you are well." Tree observed Adam's restless and shifting eyes darting behind her. He was trying to catch a glimpse of the strange creature hovering silently in the background.

Tree pacified Adam's tension and worries by providing and a proper introduction to the strange foreigner. "Adam, I would like you to meet Eve." Adam appeared skeptical. "Eve has been assigned to serve as my caretaker and aide. She is the direct reason for my hasty recovery." Eve stepped forward into light away from the shadowy dimness of Trees frame. Standing in plain sight the creature Eve appeared shy if not nervous to meet Adam, "Come Eve," Tree called out, " meet my good friend Adam, he is the one that I have been telling you about."

Adam was mesmerized by the creature's beauty. Eve's design resembled that of his mate with only a few distinctive differences. Eve was more youthful resembling a vibrant younger version of his mate. Eve's beauty and well-framed body only helped to enhance and further Adam's growing interest and attraction. The contrast of Eve beauty to the likeness of his mate was oddly flawed in the comparison. Eve resembled the epitome of perfection a creature sculpted and molded by gifted hands. Her eyes shone clear and bright like the moon in the darkest of nights. Her beauty was simply breathtaking. Her long flowing hair rested comfortably over her shoulder draping down her neck and back. Adam appeared mesmerized by the creature and stood frozen gazing over the newcomer. He examined Eve as though unable to conceive how such beauty and radiance could exist in a single being.

Adam did not speak finding his lips sealed between his teeth. His eyes studied every inch and curve of the creature's anatomy. Eve was uncertain as to the customs of introduction and breaking the awkward silence she uttered in a sweet and gentle voice. "Hello, Adam, I am Eve. I am very honored to meet you." He was astonished by the audible fact that he could hear Eve voice speaking to him. Adam was shocked somewhat ambushed by the angelic sound of Eve's voice that he could not conceive or produce a single response. He gawked in fascination and disbelief surprised to discover that the wonderful creature could also speak. It was obvious that Adam had been living too long in the silent and quiet company of his mate. He was enchanted if not overly impressed by the creature's ability to produce words and communicate effectively.

Hearing Eve speak and move about animated and free very much like himself was simply an amazing sight for Adam to behold. "Hello." Adam finally responded, "Thank you for your support in aiding Tree and helping to restore her back to her healthy self again." "No thanks necessary," Eve responded, "however you are quite welcome." She answered laughing nervously. Adam was quite fascinated with the creatures and finding muse in the creature's voice he paused to listen on, "It has been my pleasure in caring for such a noble and admirable creature such as Tree." Eve produced a smile that gleamed across her face which instantly enhanced her beauty and appearance. These simple gestures helped to further Eve's physical appeal and heighten her attraction if deemed possible. Adam found himself somewhat smitten by the caretaker and was naturally drawn by the inkling allure of curiosity and growing interest in Eve. Adam could not take his eyes off the fair damsel not even for a moment. The magnetic force of attraction and curiosity seemed to draw Adam and Eve closer to one another.

In no time at all, Adam found himself standing beside the newcomer. Eve felt strangely humbled and filled with nervousness standing before the renowned son of God. Adam engaged Eve in pleasant dialogue with hopes of developing a friendship or building rapport . "Eve is truly an appropriate name for a creature of your grace and stature." The generosity of Adams kind words and compliment caused Eve to blush uncontrollably. Despite her effort to conceal her feelings Eve was unable to hide the hue of redness that flushed over her face. Eve accepted Adams compliment and responded accordingly. "Eve befits me as perfectly as the name Adam suits you." The two creatures stood silently basking over one another. They reflected looks of marvel and astonishment amused by their very existence. The rejoicing smiles they shared with one another indicated that both Adam, and Eve were enchanted by the disposition of their newly found friendship.

It went without question that there was an unspoken attraction and chemistry building between Adam and Eve. The pair seemed suited for one another sharing similar views and outlooks on life. Tree was surprised to discover how well the two creatures faired in their interaction and engagement. Looking on at Adam and Eve one would assume that the two held a former acquaintance. Tree felt moved to speak out but understood that this interaction was all part of God's plan. She was in no position to interfere with the unfurling of her king's illustrious plot. Tree watched on in silent observation feeling somewhat annoyed by Adams disregard and dismissal of her presence. Tree did not disclose her discontent or speak out against Adam's behavior and poor display self-control. She nursed her private thoughts aside her bruised ego. Tree was learning to cope with the grief and sorrow felt internally in having betrayed her closest and dearest friend.

Throughout the duration of her recovery Tree confided in Eve expressing the depth of her woes and sorrows in having been separated from Adam. Her extended absence and time apart from Adam had taken an awkward and unexpected toll over Trees perception and judgment. During her rehabilitation Tree bolstered and spoke highly of Adam's unyielding loyalty and unwavering commitment to his family. However, now Tree was unable to look Adam directly in his face. She felt rather uneasy and burdened with of shame and guilt in colluding with God to ensnare Adam. Tree harbored the hope that space and distance would help her overcome the remorse and guilt festered deep inside. Secretly Tree hopped that Adam would never return to Eden. Though unfortunate was the circumstances of their estrangement the distance and separation would ensure that the king's grand scheme would never unfold.

Under different circumstances Adams visit to Eden would warrant a cause for joy and celebration however under present circumstances Tree was unable to celebrate Adams return. She felt conflicted with knowledge that she was coerced and used a pawn and tool to lure Adam back to Eden. Tree struggled to accept the startling revelation that her very existence had been reduced to serve as the facilitator to the perfect meet cute. She imagined herself to be an unwilling participant being used and manipulated to fulfill her masters' desires. Tree was undoubtably beginning to feel uneasy with her decision not to speak out and considered for a moment the thought of disclosing the entire hoax as a sham. A wave of emotions flooded her body feeling somewhat upset and irritated regarding the extent of her abuse. Tree was feeling neglected and ignored by her close friend while managing subjugation and oppression from her king and master.

Adam and Eve joined Tree taking their places beneath the shade of her large branches. Adam and Tree began by talking candidly with Eve to offer conventional wisdom which they found purposeful and necessary for the new creature to know. Eve being relatively new to the world around her seemed amazed and typically impressed by the vast wealth of knowledge shared their Tree and Adam. They trio talked for most of the day sharing opinions on matters of philosophy and current events taking place within the kingdom. They all took turns talking listening and laughing amongst one another. Adam, and Tree orated stories and tales filled with witty anecdotes and parables.

Tree felt compelled to tell stories of Adam's childhood sharing intimate tales detailing Adam as being a rambunctious youth. "Compared to the man before us today," Tree laughed, "Adam was quite the troublemaker." Eve was amused by Trees stories and begged to hear more joyful memories placing special interest in hearing tales that involved Adams learned mishaps experiences. Adam did not mind being the topic of discussion and did little to challenge or deter the subject. On the contrary Adam granted Tree free range to continue sharing her stories freely. He did not want to refuse Eve a moment of good humor nor would he deny himself the joy and satisfaction of hearing the angelic sound of her laughter. Even if it came at the expense and cost of his own blunder and buffoonery.

They sat together underneath Trees lofty branches enjoying the coolness of the day. Her large limbs provided shade and protection from the hot sun. Adam was honored and received recognition for his triumphant return. Many creatures came from far and wide to greet Adam and brought with them gifts. Tree gifted Adam a cornucopia of delectable fruits along with many more offerings, brought forth by the respectable inhabitants of the kingdom. The animals brought spices and herbs, roots and gingers and other various forms of vegetation. There were given and bestowed onto Adam as a collective gesture and effort from the garden. Even the hard-working honeybees took a short break buzzing by to pay their respects and homage to the returned prince. They gifted him a chunky piece of their honeycomb dripping with sweet nectar sappy dew. The celebration of Adam homecoming was met with joy and merriment. Adam was very much in good spirits enjoying the festivities and having a good time. It did not take long before Adam began to lose track of time during his enjoyment and celebration. He soon found himself lost amongst the crowd and company of familiar and unknown faces. Adam socialized with new acquaintances while rekindling old and lost friendships.

Tree playfully reminded Adam of the time with the mention of his proclivity to tardiness. "Nightfall draws near," Tree called out, "I think it would be best if begin to journey home and return with the awakening of the sun." Adam began to recover his senses. "Yes, I agree." He answered. "It is growing late, and I should return home at once." He looked over at Eve and saw that she was saddened by the announcement of his departure. "Will you return to us," Eve asked, "like you say." Adam, smiled at Eve and responding with affection in his voice, "The warm reception I received today, has truly moved me" Adam explained, "The true question now is how will I be able to keep myself away from this place; the very land I once called home." Adam bid Tree and Eve a final farewell while making declarations of a hasty return. "I will be back soon" Adam declared grabbing his basket of fruits and the remainder of his gifts. He eventually returned to the trail leading him out of Eden and back home to his family.

Adam arrived home in a particularly good mood. The image of Eve caressed his mind and nestled his thoughts. That night he could hardly rest in his bed replaying the events of his day. Adam laid awake for most of the night absorbed in delightful thoughts. He replayed the events of his day over again in his mind. In the late hours of the night Adam could be seen pacing impatiently back and forth stopping regularly to look out into the pitch-dark sky. He cursed the night stars crediting the moon as the source of his bane and troubles. The calmness and stillness of the night seem to taunt Adam incessantly. It was there that he conceived the impossible thought of one day being able to expedite and manipulate time. "Wretched darkness why not be done already and give way to the light of the flaming sun," Adam rambled on in freeform between poetic discourse and anguish. His wasted efforts to intimidate the moon soon left him feeling weary and moving about sluggishly around the room. Every few moments or so Adam would grip the bridge of his nose and rub his eyes. This action was usually followed by howling yawn. It was obvious to see that Adam was tired and exhausted however he was determined to stay awake to greet the sun. He refused to be taken down or subdued by the lethargic hands of sleep.

Adam stood against the doorway of his cavern for most of the night. It was not long before the overwhelming weight of exhaustion disabled Adam against his willful wishes. Adam was now comatose on the floor sleeping near the entranceway of his home. The sun had long risen but Adam hardly noticed the change in the day. His weary body was tired and consumed with exhaustion. Adam felt as though the stars and moon had somehow conspired against him taking offense to the onslaught of his outburst and verbal threats. The withholding retaliation of sunrise seemed to help cripple Adam into submission. The exhaustive postponement had unintentionally forced Adam into a deep state of restful sleep.

It was his Cain who discovered his father resting at the doorway and woke him. "Father!" Cain called out, "Why are you sleeping on the ground?" Adam appeared drowsy and partially disoriented at the time.

He worked quickly to collect and gather his thoughts. An image of Eve in the garden suddenly flashed into his head. The thought prompted Adam to jump onto his feet. He declared his commitment and intent to go out hunting and comb the wilderness for food. "May I come along father?" Cain asked in as supple and saddened tone. Adam felt unprepared frankly not know how to respond to his son. Adam could not produce plausible excuse to deny Cain his request to join him. However, Adam knew very well that his son could not accompany him on his journey and voyage to the secret garden.

Adam was fearful that his son would enter the sacred grounds an uncover his newly coveted secret. "No," Adam answered, "not this time. I will be brief. Notify your mother that I will return home in time for supper." Adam made the declaration without looking or waiting for his son's response. It was not long before Adam set out once again eager and ambitious in his return to the florescent and scenic world of Eden. Cain shouldered the feelings of disappointment as he watched his father walking along the barren and rocky pathway. His eyes trailed from a distance as he watched Adam walking away.

Cains image of his father began to slowly shrink as Adam furthered his descent. Stepping further away Adam was being reduced to the size of an ant in stature and size. Cain watched from afar as the frame and image of his father began to slowly diminish beneath the light of the glowing sun. It wasn't long before the image of Adam's body began to blend harmoniously into the background. Adam moved amiably through the wilderness like a man consumed with fiery desire and passion. He ventured forth in direction of his lofty pursuits wavering a false sense of urgency in his stride.

13

The Decompensation

Adam began to increase his visits Eden to see his friends Tree, and Eve and the host of colorful characters residing in Eden. His visits to the garden became more routine and frequent consisting of most of his day. Adam often took leave in the early mornings and stayed outside throughout the day returning home just before dusk. Adams family was unaware and ignorant of his secret life beyond the grand walls. His family expressed minimal scrutiny or suspicion regarding Adams conduct and behavior. They saw no reason to suspect or challenge their beloved leader. They accepted without question the summary and collection of his day. Adam started to become more distracted and withdrawn from his family and began spending less quality time at home. He seldomly engaged with his family and struggled to make and attend their evening family meals.

One evening when attending dinner in his home Adam found himself feeling somewhat annoyed and irritated by Cains incessant request to hear updated stories and tales of his father's exploits. Adam stammered and stumbled over his words exercising caution to avoid disclosing too much information. He was careful to avoid detailing the setting and location of his stories. Adam was particularly vigilant in redacting the full extent of his deeds and adventures. He decided it was best to omit any incriminating information which was deemed unnecessary from his stories.

Adams conquests as an outdoorsman was growing less reputable as Adam was more often returning home bearing only fruits and vegetation. It did not take long before his family began to observe the drastic change in Adams attitude surrounding their nutrition and wellbeing. Adam began to insist and urge that the family consider changing their current diet. The family no longer enjoyed the flame broiled protein and taste of meaty foods. But were instead being fed a daily regimen of fruits, and vegetation. These delectables Adam smuggled and brought home nightly from his returns. Adam was never home it seemed and would often return during the late hours of the night plaguing with fatigue and exhaustion.

The first night when Adam brought home delectable fruits, the delightful treat was truly a surprise. It had been a long time since his mate and child tasted the sweet, delicious nectar of ambrosia and other fruits. His family enjoyed the gifts of fruits that day and tolerated it again the second day. However, the pattern of excessive fruits and vegetation soon became problematic in their home. There were peels and spoiled remains of uneaten fruits lay scattered about the den. The scent of decaying produce began to attract small insects namely flys and pesky gnats into their home.

Adam's conspicuous faults and shortcomings were becoming increasingly observable to his family. They were starting to connect the noticeable changes and growing inconsistencies in his usual pattern and behavior. Adam could no longer dismiss or discount his absence under the guise and pretense of hunting without having anything to show. Truthfully Adam could scarcely recall the last time he gave chase after game or brought home a hefty loaf of meat to his family. It was apparent that Adam too was struggling internally with his own behavior growing more critical of the facade and false image in which he was projecting. In attempt to align his moral compass and ease the feelings of tension and guilt swelling in his heart. The feelings of remorse he harbored developed gradually over time from repeated acts of deception and deceit. It began with Adam declaring a ban and discontinuation of meats from their diet and home. He minimized the benefits of hunting and instead endorsed the many feasible benefits associated with produce and vegetation as the better alternative and much healthier choice. The substitution of their current diet demanded that vegetables were be served regularly and more plentiful during evening meals.

It came to a point that Cain began to refuse his supper as act of protest. He refused to eat from the basket of fruits and vegetation. One day at dinner Cain spoke to his father about the lingering subject. "I am sorry father" Cain apologized, "but I can no longer bare to eat these foods." He refused the plate of salad before him pushing the meal away. "We have been eating vegetables and fruits for more than a fortnight as I can recall." Adam dismissed his son concerns with a lighthearted laughter and a jovial sneer. "Do not be ridiculous son," Adam answered. "These natural foods offer protein and energy serving as a source nutrition." "We do not care about the benefits father," Cain responded sharply. "Fruits and vegetation are good and well however they leave much to be desired in substance and taste." Cain seemed genuinely confused looking over his father in face. "Why do you no longer bring home game and prey like before?" Cain inquired posing the question to his father. "You no longer bring home the foods that we like or enjoy."

Adam felt confronted by his son's demand growing rather annoyed and upset by Cains newly found sense of audaciousness. His inquisitions began to make Adam feel uneasy and uncomfortable as he responded defensively. "Do you think it is easy to set out daily in search for game or make prey of large sized beasts without being exposed to susceptible harm." Unable to face his son Adam looked down at his feet as he spoke unable to accept the beaten brows of skepticism drawn over his son's face. The offensive insult reminded Adam of his own falsehood and shortcomings. "If you think yourself better than I." Adam boasted, "Then go forth, and bring home the meat and foods in which you seek to devour." Adam concluded harshly slamming his fist on the table. The unexpected action sent the remains of his meal food flying into the air.

Hot tempered and annoyed by the blundering act, Adam remained unfazed or undeterred by the pressing outcome. Leering directly into the face of his son with a fierce and somewhat intimidating gaze. Cain appeared unnerved by his father's forceful glare; however, he refused to allow Adam's anguish and rage to deter him from accepting the proposal. "I will!" Cain sharply countered accepting his father challenge. The flare of Cains boiling temper was typically observed during the peak stages of early adolescent. Still and all Adam was surprised and somewhat taken aback by the exuberant display of contemptuous arrogance his Cain's tone in addressing and speaking with him.

"I will!" Shouted the young lad, "I shall hunt and slay the largest and wildest of beasts and haul the carcass home so that we may enjoy a proper and sensible meal." Cain was highly upset his temper led him to remove himself from the small dining area prematurely without requesting or obtaining permission. In one angry swooping motion Cain moved from dining area into the comfortable lounge and living room area where he now kept bed. His nerves quaked violently against the throbbing rhythm of his drumming heartbeat. Unable to tame or control his nerves and composure Cain began to weep silently until finally he turned over and fell into a deep sleep.

Adam's mate sat in silent concern seeming very much torn and afflicted by the growing tension between Adam and Cain. The look of displeasure worn by his partner seem to disagree and condemn Adam for his rash behavior and ill temper. His partner offered silent gestures encouraging Adam to pursue a path of recourse in following up with their son, however Adam did not respond. Somehow without having to look up at his mate Adam could feel the pulsating heat radiating from his partner's fiery gaze. Adam ignored the sweltering urge and temptation to react and defend his delinquent behavior. Adam behaved evasively and somewhat arrogant in his refusal to meet the annoyed face of his partner. He instead diverted his gaze and attention elsewhere into opposite direction.

Adam remained stubbornly committed in his arrogance and unwillingness to accept fault or accountability for the mishap that just occurred. He excused himself moving quietly from his dinner seat into his lounge chair. Adam avoided crossing paths with his mate unwilling at the time to bear the look of disappointment drawn across his partner face. Adam sat down to rest his mind and body feeling somewhat upset and annoyed at the entire ordeal that just transpired. In his current state of passive anguish Adam was unwilling to consider his conduct or take any accountability for his behavior. He refused to accept a hand in the matter and was now choosing indifference as his moderator and defense. The burden of guilt and shame that coiled his nerves caused Adam to bite his tongue at times and seal his lips. He held false hope in the belief that withholding communication would somehow exonerate him from having to provide a reasonable explanation for his conduct. The silent condemnation of Adam seemed to be the only appropriate response. Adam committed to the belief that no amount of reasoning or explanation could suffice in liberating him of his wrongdoings. He proceeded to lay his head and body down alongside the host of judgements that caroled his mind and occupied his thoughts. It did not take long before those same straggling thoughts carried him off to sleep.

The next morning as Adam set forth on his departure he observed his son Cain. The young man still appeared upset as he geared up to hunt and scavenge for food. Cain appeared eager in not determined to prove to his father that he too was capable of fending and providing for the family. The young lad was puny in stature and structure however he made up for it with strength and ambition. Cains demeanor resembled that of a proud warrior walking tall with his face to the sky. Adorned in the latest primal attire designed with safety in mind Cain looked ready to embark on a monumental task and undertaking.

Unbeknown to Adam at the time, Cain was growing rather skilled in the art of crafting. He adopted the hobby of forging several lethal tools and accessories. Cain opposed to his father's use of the term "tools," and instead coined his variation of sharp and deadly instruments as "weapons." He did so in describing their lethal capability and efficiency in helping to bring down prey. Over his shoulders Cain now carried his father's abandoned satchel after modifying the old tool bag to fit his small body and frame. Cain resembled the striking image and likeness of his father geared up with his bag slung confidently over his shoulders. Heavily draped in scavenger linen Cain began his descent chartering through the merciless wilderness to find and hunt down game.

Cain retained the inherent advantage and intellect which he inherited from his parents. The fact that Cain was identical to his father also meant that he too harnessed the powers of wit and imagination like his creators. Cain was gifted and favorably blessed with intelligence and ingenuity. His strong will and determination would become a defining trait and trademark that would be adopted by the decedents of his lineage. Cain held a natural knack for conjuring up effective and resourceful weapons which he created and crafted specifically for slaying and bringing down wild beasts.

Cain was resourceful and able to erect complex traps for his prey. He often resorted to digging ditches and holes than filling the base with stakes and spikes which he personally sharpened and forged. Cain molded and bended various materials to his will until they formed the perfect weapon to snag his prey and quickly make easy sport of the formidable beasts. It went without saying that Cains insightful skills of craftsmanship and forgery went unmatched. Each passing day was another chance for him to improve his craft. What Cain lacked in size and strength he made up for with sharp wit and intellect. Despite facing numerous blunders and failed attempts did was not derailed or detoured from the path of his growing ambitions. Cain would not allow let the mocking gaze of his father's brows discourage him from achieving his objective. His will was mighty but stronger was his determination to prove himself worthy and deserving of his father's admiration and love.

Cain worked tirelessly to improve his hunting technique and scavenging skills. He hunted daily working nonstop until finally he succeeded in capturing and slaying his first prey. The savage beast was a rather rugged beast of medium proportion and size. Though his capture appeared small in comparison to the heftier savages that his father slayed Cain still rejoiced. It was true that Adam brought home larger beasts and creatures of prey in his hunt and outings. However, even so with that being the case Cain refused to allow the competitive spirit of jealousy and spite to ruin the joyful moment. Cain was enthralled with excitement at the grand feat of his accomplishment. For the first time in his life, he had slain a beast alone without the support and assistance of his father.

Cain celebrated by jumping up and down dancing around the pit hole cleverly dug to ensnare its victim by plummeting to death. Cain managed to retrieve the beast from of the hole by way of tossing the beast back up to the ground. He swelled with immense pride and was eager to return home and furnish the outcome of his good fortune. He looked forward to his mother's warm reception which he imagined would be filled with affection and affirmation. Cain planned to turn the beast over to his mother for treatment and preparation. He requested that the tusks of the small boorish beast be retained to serve as a testimonial token to his crowning achievement. The monumental occasion would symbolize Cains a monumental transition and transformation into adulthood. Cains mother appeared surprised by the astonishing out of his endeavors. His mother swelled with immense pride and pleasure and was happily accepting of Cains offer with gratitude.

Both mother and child appeared filled with excitement. The two moved quickly to prepare a celebratory meal in anticipation of Adam's return. They worked together in perfect harmony to prepare a delicious meal for the family to enjoy. They seasoned and cooked the food to Adams preference and liking ensuring that extra portions of salad and vegetation was placed on his plate. Cain and his mother were proud of them-selves and happily awaited Adam return. They waited and waited but Adam did not arrive home at his usual time. The meal began to grow cold and soggy. The warm delicious dinner no longer held the same enticing aroma or appeal.

Cain was growing impatiently weary but kept him-self awake hoping to catch a glimpse of his father's face. He relished over the look of astonishment and surprise his father would wear at receiving such a joyful reception. Cain was filled with excitement in his father learning of his great feat and accomplishment. It was not until the approach of dusk that Adam arrived home and entered the lofty den. He was surprised and somewhat caught off guard to find his mate and child eagerly awaiting his arrival. His family allowed Adam a brief moment to settle down and decompress. The routine itself consisted of Adam changing and removing his outside clothing and settling into more comfortable attire. Adam began to sense the trailing gaze of his family's glare. The supportive duo began to question Adams actions and movements, growing oddly suspicious of his whereabouts. Adam caught sight of the finely prepared dinner and quickly took offense to the elaborately home cooked meal.

Adam was intentionally critical in his observation of the splendid feast. He deliberately declared his appetite as having instantly subsided. He saw the meal as an affront and attack on his character bringing into questioned his ability to provide and lead his family. Adam saw the gesture as an attempt to undermine his authority and minimize his rank and status. He refused to sit down and eat of any foods or meal having been cooked and prepared by the contemptuous hands of his son. It was safe to assume that Adam was not pleased and was in no way happy with the surprise dinner. Adam misplaced his anger somehow perverted his view of thoughtful dinner as an indignant affront and act of defiance. He carried a false security in accepting the distorted belief that the meal was in some way was intended to serve as a symbol of mockery. Adam was adamant and utterly convinced that the food placed before him was put there to belittle and diminish his character. While helping to elevate Cains rank and position to a higher tier in the dynamic family composition.

Cain waited patiently for his father's recognition and praise. However, when no praise came, Cain diminished his standards to accept any form recognition or acknowledgment for the well-prepared meal that he and his mother had proudly slaved over. Adam did not speak but moved about casually through the room with an air of arrogance in his strut. Cain and his mother watched with swelling eagerness and excitement as

Adam moved closer to the dining area in view of the large feast placed before him. Adam sat poised for a moment looking over his meal with discerning gaze. He appeared annoyed and riddled with countless questions. He was unsure how to appropriately respond to the celebratory demotion and sanctioning. Adam struggled internally fighting back the urge to push the meal and food off the table. He emerged from his shadowy thoughts with a menacing smile. He instantly began to ravish away at the food eating every morsel on his plate but deliberately leaving the meat and main dish untouched. He ate in silence never once lifting his head to look up to meet the annoyed faces of his family looking down on him.

Cain watched his father with an irritable anguish growing and festering deep within him. Adam finished his meal and calmly rose to his feet. Without expressing a gesture of gratitude Adam walked over quietly to the bed and laid his weary body down to rest. Cain and his mother were astonished by Adams behavior and looked on at him with loathing irritation and confusion. They were somewhat disappointed by Adams shameful display of disregard and disrespect. The grimacing smirk he wore across his face mocked and perplexed the confused onlookers. Adam belched loudly before giving out a howling yawn. He stretched out his arms before folding them comfortably behind his head to rest his eyes. It did not take very long before Adam fell into a deep state of sleep.

Cain was truly heartbroken by his father's actions. The wound of witnessing Adams disregard and neglect seemed to scar and wound him deeply. Adam was perversely fulfilling his darkest fear by losing the esteem and regard of his partner and son. Cain appeared unsettled and felt as though he had been ambushed by a swarm of painful emotions. The intense feelings hit hard for Cain almost as if he had been struck forcefully in the chest. Cain had never experienced such rapid flood of emotions. His blood and temper boiled feverishly while his nerves and veins ran chilling cold. The combination of anguish and pain prompted tears of frustration to spew slowly from corners of his eyes. Cain feelings as well as his pride were hurt by the fact that his father was committed to making a mockery and spectacle of him. That night Cain did not speak but followed the example of his elder and took himself bed. Adam's mate witnessing the entire ordeal was highly upset by Adams behavior. The troubled creature was unable follow behind Adam and Cain's path to rest. The lonely matriarch sulked silently through the midnight hours weeping pensively over of the ensuing degradation and the possible demolition of their family and home.

To Be Continued....

Prince Otchere is a contemporary African author with deep spiritual and religious ties to the Christian apologetic faith. His eclectic style of writing and storytelling is uniquely tailored to Christ conscious readers, and those seeking spiritual wisdom, understanding. Prince writes religiously with the intention of liberating audiences and followers from post-modern ideology that inhibit spiritual growth and development. Raised predominantly in the Christian faith, Prince draws his inspiration from the Genesis story and now looks to add meaning and depth to the classic biblical story and historical tale. Prince has professional experience in the field of behavioral mental health with a master's level education in the field of Social Work. Prince is a visionary writer whose profound works offers conventional gems of wisdom as well as guidance to readers through his unique style of writing and storytelling. Prince draws his insight from a combination of spaces including social, personal, professional and spiritual life. An author and a collector of human experiences, Prince possesses the keen skills of observation and empathy which he utilizes in his interpretation and retelling of famous historical events and stories. Prince is an existentialist writer who work explore parallels between human experience and religious ideology which governs human behavior. Prince writes candidly to his audience in a genuine and authentic narrative that helps to highlight the integrity and truth of his message. Prince has an empathetically unique writing style that allows him to channel his imagination and senses beyond the boundaries of space and time.

www.ingramcontent.com/pod-product-compliance
Lightning Source LLC
Chambersburg PA
CBHW071125100726
47908CB00008B/2493